CALVIN PARTRIDGE

Entity Endgame

Cover Images:

Earth from NASA, missiles from U.S. Navy, girl from Steve Pepple via BigStockPhoto.com

First edition

ISBN: 978-1-8384906-1-4

This book was professionally typeset on Reedsy.
Find out more at reedsy.com

Dedicated to the Dengue Fever infected mosquito that confined me to bed long enough to begin writing, and to Sarah for the enthusiasm that kept me going.

Contents

1

Extraordinary

There was something supernatural here, something extraordinary.

At first sight there was nothing unusual; an old man looking up at an old temple in central Myanmar, still known to many by its old name, Burma. However the building looming over him housed a mystery. Centuries ago three of its inner chambers had been filled with loose bricks covering whatever lay inside. Until archaeologists could raise sufficient funds from their disinterested, authoritarian government to fund excavations a mystery it would remain. But it wasn't the temple that was extraordinary.

It lay on a dry, dusty plain beyond the crumbling walls of the ancient city of Bagan. Intermittent patches of shrubs caked brown by months of wind driven dust eddies waited patiently for the start of the rains. No homes or farm buildings were to be found but the plain was far from empty. Crowding within just a few kilometres were more than 4,500 temples, peppering the landscape. It made for a mind boggling sight, but it wasn't the plain that was extraordinary either. It was the old man.

He stood out in front, blinking in the sharp light and sharper heat of the early afternoon sun. His white beard appeared to be trying to emulate Hemmingway's but instead looked more like Gandalf's might after being attacked by a blunt pair of shears. His gnarled, polished walking stick added to a wizardly appearance but his bold features and dark shade of skin suggested an origin within the Middle East, not Middle Earth.

Outwardly he was a typical tourist, looking and feeling out of place. However to the hordes of vendors there were surprises. Firstly he was on foot, whereas tourists invariably explored the plain by bicycle or horse and cart. Secondly he was talking out loud, apparently to himself.

"I'm not disputing this is the place, but it just doesn't... look right, you know".

Most surprising of all was the fact he had almost made it to the entrance without any of them spotting his approach. A puzzling oversight but one easily remedied. The hawker boys descended on him en masse.

"Hey mister, what country you from?"

"Hello. Well I was born in Egypt, though strictly speaking..." the old man started.

"Good country Egypt - it's got pyramids," a boy informed him as if the man did not know. "You want to buy a postcard?"

"No, I have no money."

"You want change money? Good rate!"

"No, I won't be purchasing anything from any of you, thank you very much," the old man said politely and unequivocally, but it did nothing to deter them.

"You want to buy a carving? Look. Very nice," ventured another boy.

Hawkers were something he was familiar with from Egypt, but even experienced travellers know it is impossible to deter the most persistent. In his experience a firm response early on was the only hope.

He turned towards them and said forcefully, "No, and I would be grateful if you could all now leave me in peace to explore."

"Yes, very peaceful here. You want to buy postcard to remember?"

Ignoring them he moved inside, only to have more boys join the throng and repeat the same ineffective sales pitches. When his lack of response did nothing to relieve the onslaught he tried reasoning with them instead but to no avail. With his options exhausted he became increasingly exasperated. Did they really believe if they asked the same question enough times they would get a different answer?

He pushed past them into the first chamber. Enough daylight streamed in from the large entrance way to reveal a stone statue of the Buddha.

"Single Buddha," said one boy hoping for a guide's tip. The old man fled to the next chamber with the boys racing after him and jostling one another like the turbulent wake behind a ship. In it were two Buddha images representing the past and future of Buddhism. A fact unknown to the would-be tour guide.

"Two Buddhas," he announced unhelpfully. "Think you want postcard of them sending to your family?"

Something snapped inside. Even at the best of times it would have been an unfortunate question to ask the man, if a man he still was, and with his patience exhausted it was far from the best of times.

"May I?" he asked.

The question had not been directed to any one of the boys in particular, rather to a space somewhere just above their heads. Before any of them could check if the man meant he wanted to examine their wares events drove the unspoken query from their lips.

One moment a tired looking old man stood before them, the next only his outline remained. Where his body had been there was a window onto another place in a different time.

A hot desert sun blazed down on a giant Egyptian pyramid swarming with workers. The polished white limestone facing was almost complete and it made an impressive sight, crowned with a gold top resplendent in reflected sunlight. The view swept inwards to focus on a much younger but very familiar foreman. He was directing and urging on a group of workers who were struggling to control a limestone block hanging precariously from a web of ropes.

The old man spoke with a harshness, clarity and volume not previously present.

"How old do you think I am? Seventy? Eighty? I was born over four millennia ago. I have seen wonders and tragedies. I have watched empires rise and fall."

The view changed dizzyingly between events and countries, battles being fought, cities growing and burning.

"But I left behind everything and everyone I ever loved including my wife and three children for this friendless, endless existence." His voice began to trail off, his thoughts drifting. "I don't belong here, I don't belong anywhere any more..."

Suddenly the window was gone and the old man's body snapped back into view, and with it his focus.

"So no," he said with sudden, sharp steel in his voice, "I don't want a postcard to send to my long dead family."

The boys had all been rooted to the floor in shock. Now they remembered their legs and fled as one.

"Thank you for indulging me," said the man.

"No problem. In my experience big stories from little children are seldom believed."

Just then a pair of tourists turned into the chamber from the inner walkway. Seeing him alone some of the gaggle of vendors peeled away from the harassed looking couple and ran up to him.

"Hey mister where you from? You wanna buy postcard?"

He sighed. "You know, I don't think we are going to learn much here. I haven't seen any priests around. Let's try India instead; I hear they have gurus there who may be able to help. We could start with Delhi. Hopefully we'll get less hassle there too."

"Very well."

The old man ambled slowly out and away from the temple onto the plain. A man born long before the earliest temple on that plain had been conceived. An extraordinary man.

He walked until no more eyes were upon him, then his body broke up into thousands of pieces each of which immediately broke up into millions, until they were too small to see and he was gone.

2

The Beginning

And God said, Let there be light: and there was light.
[Genesis 1:3]

To tell the story properly it needs to be told from the beginning.
Not just any beginning - The Beginning.

In the beginning there was nothing. The universe was not
black, it was not empty, it simply did not exist. There was no
void where it would one day be, there was not even such a thing
as time.

And then there was light.

An entire universe appeared in a space much, much smaller
than a pin prick. Nobody knows where it came from and indeed
it may even be unknowable.

At first it was a strange quantum place where even the most
basic laws of physics did not exist, but by the time it was a
trillionth of a second old it had started to settle down and a
seething soup of elementary particles began to emerge.

What seems surprising at first is that there was also life, not
just some life but teeming multitudes of simple organisms that

quickly emerged from clumps of gluon linked quarks. On reflection it seems less surprising and more inevitable. An entire universe of particles buzzed around and interacted with each other. Most connected and broke apart to no effect but inevitably the sheer scale of the unimaginably massive universe meant again and again they randomly fell into combinations that provided building blocks for a form of life, though quite unlike what was to follow.

The environment was changing furiously fast and species were rapidly wiped out, though for a while new ones continued to be created in the intense, swirling furnace.

Only the more complex organisms had any chance of surviving for more than a split second, and that depended very much on their strategies. Some sought merely to exist and in doing so they died. Others reproduced by cloning themselves, with more sophisticated versions introducing random changes or requiring two organisms to encourage mutations. It was a strategy which was to work well in a much older universe but here they could not adapt fast enough to the changing environment and all eventually perished.

The most successful one chose simply to grow, connecting itself to its neighbouring particles and arranging them in a copy of itself, but crucially it maintained a link between parent and child rather than simply making an independent clone. Due to the tiny distances involved growth was swift and exponential. Although there was no strategy behind it the network layout it formed effectively created a neural net, so as it grew to an ever greater size it gained first intelligence and then self awareness.

Its first significant thought was the realisation that both it and the universe would be dead before the first second was up. The problem was that matter and anti-matter were present in equal quantities, with the entity happening to be a creature of the latter. Unfortunately when one came into contact with the other both were annihilated in a colossal explosion, sending more particles of matter and anti-matter crashing into one another in chain reactions that ripped through the tiny universe.

Soon there would be nothing left and both entity and universe would be no more.

3

Underground

For a moment Alex was disorientated, not knowing where she was. A hard, gritty floor pressed against her cheek. Her hearing had been affected by something and what little she could hear was disturbing. There were moans and then at last one, almost tentative, scream found voice then trailed off uncertainly as if embarrassed.

She opened her eyes which she had no recollection of closing. It made little difference though a flickering yellow light revealed just enough for memories to come flooding back, forcing their way through the numbing shock.

She had been on a London tube train and still was for that matter, but the comfortable soporific clickaty-clack that had started to lull her to sleep had been torn away by a blaze of light and two mighty jolts before the darkness swept in. There had been some kind of explosion, maybe a bomb. Not in her carriage but not far away.

The second jolt had been the most violent, hurling passengers from their seats as the derailed carriages crashed into an obstruction ahead, perhaps the collapsed tunnel if it had indeed been a bomb. Looking up she realised the only illumination was coming from fires outside the carriage and even that was beginning to be obscured by smoke, an orange dimming light pulsating darkly through its folds.

Her first instinct was to get up and run but the words of her adrenaline sports nut brother came to her unbidden.

"If ever you feel rising panic STOP. Don't act. Panicking people always grab at the first solution they can think of. It's unlikely to be the best one and you may only get one chance. Stop and list your options, the few seconds it takes will pay off, believe me." She did believe him so she cautiously got to her feet and looked around. For four, maybe five, long seconds she looked and considered before finally choosing to run towards the flickering light of the flames and the next carriage.

It was still tenuously connected but lay on its side leaving the connecting door too low for anyone to pass through. The fire was outside but smoke was billowing in and even as she looked fingers of flame licked towards her, seeking to do the same. She grabbed the handle and with adrenaline-fuelled strength managed to slide the buckled door mostly shut. Almost all the windows featured a dense network of spider web like cracks but the toughened glass was largely whole, so her action should buy them a little time.

Once again she looked around before acting and was glad she did as fortune smiled on her. The door of a broken cabinet hung open nearby. On the cracked glass the word 'Emergency' was spelt out in large red letters and inside she could see a flashlight, fire extinguisher and first aid kit. There was no way she could put out the rapidly building fire with one extinguisher and there was no time to give people first aid even if she knew how, but she gratefully grabbed the flashlight and ran back.

All the injuries in her carriage would be due to the impact rather than the explosion. She knew the smoke would soon become a killer. "More people die from smoke than fire". Where had she heard that?

The able bodied were starting to scramble away. Somebody had managed to get the far door open and they started dropping down onto the tracks. The wrongness of it caused her a sudden surge of irritation. Switching on the flashlight produced a piercing shaft of light in smoke and dust filled gloom and she began snapping out orders. Their eyes blinded by smoke and the flashlight in her hand the carriage occupants responded to the authority in her voice, grateful for somebody who knew what to do. By the time she was close enough for them to realise the instructions were coming from a slight, 14 year old girl they had already started to obeying her directions and the moment to challenge her authority had passed.

She teamed up two able bodied people to carry out each injured passenger. Three people were left over so she assigned one each to those carrying the heaviest loads so they could be substituted as needed. Some screamed as they were picked up but Alex urged them on as she was sure both smoke and flame would spread rapidly in the confined tunnel. There was no time to splint or bandage.

Once down on the tracks the visibility was much worse and the temperature noticeably hotter. A movement above her just on the edge of her vision caught her attention. Looking up she was horrified to see that while the flames had not progressed far down the tunnel at ground level the roof of the tunnel was a different matter. Forked streams of fire were moving ever onward like a serpents tongue seeking its prey, starting to overtake them.

Alex kept her torch low where the smoke was thinner to extend its range and lit the way down the tunnel, shouting to everyone to get moving. Their progress was frustratingly slow at first but they managed to gradually increase the pace as they became accustomed to their loads and the best way to carry them. She kept glancing up and back. So far they were managing to stay ahead of the flames. Continuing to do so depended on keeping up this pace and ignoring the tiredness soaking into their limbs.

Their eyes smarted from the acrid smoke and they coughed constantly but futilely as their lungs battled endlessly to clear the fumes from their bodies.

The footing was a treacherous mix of rail and sleepers, hard to discern in the low contrast gloom. One young woman with a broken ankle had her arms over the shoulders of two men who were carrying her in a sitting position between them. One of the men tripped on a sleeper and they all went down in a tangle of limbs, with the woman letting out a shriek of pain. Alex resisted the impulse to rush over as she lacked the strength to be of much use physically and her flashlight would contribute far more than her hands could. Instead she shouted for two of her spare bodies to assist and they quickly got the trio back on their feet. The woman was gasping through gritted teeth and the rest of the group paused in shared concern but Alex urged them on again. So far they were keeping ahead of the flames but Alex was increasingly worried about the smoke and how much longer they might last before being overcome.

They walked on through the toxic gloom for what felt like an eternity but was probably only minutes. There was no words spoken, just endless unhealthy coughing.

The tunnel started curving into a gradual left turn. She

glanced behind to check on the flames. Only a dull, ominous, orange/red glow was visible through the billowing blackness making it hard to judge distance or intensity. She looked forward again and was horrified to see another glow through the smoke ahead. She felt the panic she had worked so hard to control launch upwards from her stomach. Was there another fire in front of them? If so they were surely doomed.

Then she realised the colour was different, it was from white electric lighting rather than the dark, lava coloured glow behind them. As they walked on eventually the welcome sight of Oxford Street tube station came into view ahead, along with the equally welcome sight of rescuers running towards them. It was too soon for the regular emergency services to have arrived, these were station staff and transport police but they had broken open the emergency stores and were equipped with smoke hoods, lights, extinguishers and first aid kits.

They took over carrying the wounded and helped them all towards the station. Before allowing herself to be led she stood in front of a man who looked as if he was in charge and said as sharply and clearly as she could, "We are all from the last carriage, there may be others still alive but we couldn't reach them." He nodded and ran on barking orders.

The weary passengers paused for a while on the platform where the smoke was much thinner. It was empty of other passengers as the station had been closed and was being evacuated. The rescuers administered first aid and broke open stretchers ready to carry out the injured.

Exhausted more mentally than physically she put her head between her folded legs, arms wrapped around. She knew there would be a reaction setting in soon, her limbs would tremble and already she could feel a sharp prickling behind her eyes that suggested tears were not far away.

"Very impressive," said a voice beside her. She looked up and into the steady, aquamarine eyes of an old man. "Are you always that calm under pressure?"

"I don't know. That was my first and hopefully last time."

"Oh I fear not," he said with sadness.

There was something very odd about him. Unlike everybody else he lacked so much as a smudge of dirt and his clothes did not reek of smoke.

"Do you know anything about religion?" he asked unexpectedly. "I never got past god-kings myself but apparently they are out of fashion now. I tried but the temple at Bagan was a failure and Delhi... well the less said about Delhi the better."

Alex was struggling with the conversation. Normally she always had a snappy answer on hand for everyone and everything but the traumatic events seemed to have turned her wit to treacle. Temporarily lacking any smart replies she answered simply for once in her life. "We have Religious Studies lessons at school, though it's not exactly my best subject."

"Excellent. That will get you off to a flying start." Then his expression of satisfaction changed to one filled with sadness and sympathy. Suddenly he looked a lot older. Putting a hand on her shoulder he lent down and looked directly into her eyes. "I would like to tell you it's a blessing and you will learn the secrets of the universe. You will, but it is far more of a burden than a gift. The weight of the world will be on your young shoulders. I wish there was another way but I'm afraid the task is now beyond me. Good luck. You are going to need it."

She had not been able to see any physical marks on him but clearly he had suffered mentally. She turned to call for help but at that moment the entire tube station and everybody in it fragmented before her eyes, dissolving into a darkness blacker than night.

4

Chattanooga

Deep in America's rural south, near the buckle of the Bible Belt, lies the city of Chattanooga. A visiting firebrand preacher was taking a break at the Revival Meeting held in his honour and had opened up the stage to any who wanted to add their voices of support. Right now a smartly dressed man on the podium was doing so with passion, his faith burning with a clarity he wanted to share. A burning that had pushed his beliefs way beyond the safe, timid teachings of the conventional church of his youth, and he was far from alone. His thick red beard did little to cover the intense expression etched into his face.

"It's not aid the Africans want," he stated forcefully. "They don't want money or medicine or education. Jesus is coming. He's on his way. I'm not talking centuries, and I don't mean years. Months maybe, weeks more likely, and it may even be days. I don't know. What I do know is what the third world is desperate for, what they want, what they need, is *these*," he declared triumphantly, holding a bible high above his head. Whistles, whoops, shouts of "Yes, sir" and "You tell it" showed the crowd were behind him.

"I'm not saying spend less, I'm saying spend it where it is needed. So I urge those of us in positions of influence, and I know there are many, to do their utmost to see that money is not wasted on aid but redirected to good evangelical missionary churches so that we can get the Word to them before it is too late." Then he left the platform to resounding applause and claps on the back as he returned to his seat.

Another man rushed forward to take his place and add his message to the others. Grabbing the microphone he looked suddenly hesitant, as if he could not quite believe what he had done. Realising there was no turning back he took a deep breath and said, "Hello. My name is Professor Dalton, um... Richard Dalton that is."

Near the back a man by the name of Ralph sat up in his seat. He looked at the man holding the microphone and sensed trouble. He did indeed have a scholarly appearance, wearing clothes that looked like absent minded afterthoughts, as if he always had more important things on his mind. That was the first warning sign. Ralph had seen academics over-analysing religion, learning facts while losing faith. The second was that his clipped tones revealed a British accent, and Ralph knew their movement had only a very limited following in that country.

"I'd just like to ask the previous esteemed speaker whether his views on money, medicine and education apply to his own life or just the third world?" The audience were uncertain where this was going and looked uneasy.

"Has he given up his own job and taken his children out of school so they can all gain extra time to read the bible for the 'final days'? Has he cancelled his family's medical insurance? After all what is the point when there is so little time left? Has he given all his money to the church because he has more than he needs for the next few weeks?" The preacher had not been idle, he had grabbed his own microphone and now flipped the switch passing control of the speaker system away from the professor.

"We have an unbeliever among us. How sad."

Shouting now to make up for the loss of amplification the professor called out, "Or are you and everyone here hypocrites with one rule for yourselves and another for everybody else?"

A group of men gathered around him and gently but very firmly started to propel him off the stage and out of the hall.

"What happened to free speech?" he yelled.

"Oh it's alive and well and you can practice it in the parking lot outside," said the preacher to a chorus of laughter, the congregation relieved that he had taken charge, certain of the clever encouraging words they knew would soon follow to dispel any doubt.

The professor managed one last shouted question, "Do you only preach to the converted?" before the double doors at the exit swung shut and finally put an end to his barracking.

"We know the fate of the saved," said the preacher ignoring his final jibe, "and we know the fate of the sinners and the unbelievers. It fills me with sorrow. So let us not mock him or hate him. Let us all bow our heads and pray he sees the light before it is too late."

Near the back Ralph knew the professor's final jibe was a misunderstanding. Preaching to the converted was not wasted effort, far from it. The faithful brought along a never ending trickle of curious newcomers along to hear the message. In the charged atmosphere of the big hall with a convincing orator moved by God and surrounded by their enthusiastic peers the curious became intrigued, the intrigued became converted, and the converted became zealots for the cause. He was here because he loved the feeling of affirmation. He could feel his spiritual batteries recharging, filling him with an impatient eagerness to return to the fight.

Lifting his head he looked around the hall at all the people praying and his heart went out to them. They had only the words of the bible and the church to give them courage, putting up with the snide comments of Satan's sceptics trying to cast the seed of doubt in their minds. Despite that they were unwavering believers and he loved them for it. They had only faith to sustain them whereas he had the advantage of knowing. They thought that Christ was coming soon to end the world and judge them, whereas he knew it. He knew it because God had told him in no uncertain terms, and he would have accepted that even without the miracles.

The first of the miracles had been the greatest. It felt a lifetime ago but in truth only 17 months had passed since that fateful day when everything had changed. He had been sitting down watching TV, his life satisfactory but slightly lacking in direction. An ordinary, single 22 year old man on an ordinary day.

With his fair hair and square jaw Ralph was handsome enough to attract the attention of several women from his church, but he preferred not to date at random, waiting instead for some subtle sign from God to indicate who it should be. But when God spoke to him it was nothing to do with women, and it was not a quiet whisper but an explosive roar.

Suddenly there had been nothing but dust obscuring his vision and sharp edges under his body. It took a long time for the dust to settle enough to see, and a lot longer to comprehend what had happened. An enormous gas explosion had ripped through his rented house completely demolishing it, tearing into those on both sides. He was lying on top of the rubble, completely unscathed.

Much later the fire service uncovered another body in the wreckage. They were sure it was arson and this was likely to be the culprit but the DNA sample taken before the cremation had somehow become hopelessly compromised with the lab returning a result that would have been amusing in other circumstances - it was Ralph himself.

At the time he had slowly stood up, checked himself over and found to his amazement he had not a scratch on him. Then God had sent an archangel to tell him that he was right, the Second Coming was close, the world was about to end and be judged, and that he was God's chosen instrument to bring it about.

or could such a behemoth as the original parent exist.

As the first few seconds of the universe passed the entities were forced to constantly adapt, changing the makeup of their bodies as leptons briefly tried to restart the matter/anti-matter battle, neutrinos ceased interacting, and new particles such as hydrogen atoms became available for them to make upgrades. Compared to the early desperate struggle for survival the problems were straightforward and as time passed the pace of change slowed.

The universe flooded outwards at great speed scattering the population of entities throughout its vast expanse.

6

France

The tube station and everything in it had dissolved into blackness, and then the blackness dissolved again into blue. After a moment Alex realised there were white patches across it. She appeared to be lying down on her back looking up into a late summer sky. It was impossible of course. In twisting round to call for help for the old man she must have fainted, falling onto her back and probably banging her head into the bargain.

She closed her eyes and concentrated hard on what must really be there, hidden behind her delusion. She pictured the curved, rather dirty tiles of the tube station that ought to be above her. She imagined the sounds of shocked voices, the gentle wailing of the injured and the reassuring voices of the rescuers, and then she opened her eyes. There was nothing overhead but blue sky dotted with a few small cumulus clouds. A pair of birds flitted across her vision as if to rub it in.

Puzzled more than worried she sat up slowly and looked around. She was in a rather pleasant meadow and it felt very real. She could feel the heat of the sun on her skin contrasting with a cooling breeze brushing her arms and toying with her hair. She could smell freshly crushed grass, blades of which were tickling her hands and ankles.

This has to be a dream she insisted. The trouble was she didn't believe it. When people dream they *think* they are awake, but when they are awake they *know* it and she knew this was real.

Then another possibility occurred to her. She had fainted as they were being evacuated. They had been carried out to a London park to await the arrival of the ambulances, which had picked the others up but somehow left her behind. It was a nice theory and one she was loath to let go but she had to admit there were two problems with it. Firstly, looking around there were fields as far as the eye could see and there are no parks near Oxford Street that big. Secondly it had been raining hard in London before she had ducked down into the Underground with no sign of abating.

She stood up cautiously and checked herself over. Her fingers had been slightly burnt on the hot metal of the train door when she slid it shut, though she had been unaware of it at the time. She had also picked up a couple of scratches, one of which still oozed a drop of blood suggesting little time had passed. Her clothes smelt of smoke and had picked up patches of dirt but were otherwise in good condition, as was she.

Alex turned slowly on the spot doing one complete rotation. Nobody was in sight but she could see distant farm buildings and lines of trees in several directions that suggested hidden roads. Regardless of how she had come to be here getting back was going to involve a lengthy walk.

"*Hello,*" said a voice; loudly, clearly, distinctly, close by. She whipped round searching for the source but there was nobody there.

"Er... hello," she ventured back, feeling rather foolish.

"I hope I waited long enough. The Old Man said I had to give you time to adjust."

The voice didn't seem to come from any one direction; it was as if she were wearing headphones.

"Where are you? What old man?"

"We are one. The Old Man is the one you met in the underground station."

Still whipping round trying to tell which direction the voice was coming from a hundred questions bubbled to her lips all trying to get asked at once. After stammering helplessly for a moment she took a deep breath, counted to three, and decided to start with, "Where am I?"

"A field in northern France."

"France? How did I get here?"

"I brought you here."

"Why?"

"It was raining in England. All the fields there were wet."

Hmmm. She tried another tack, "Where precisely are you?"

"I am inside you. We are one."

Now that was creepy. That flash of panic she had felt in the Tube jumped back out of her stomach and up to her chest. Too much had happened in too short a space of time. She was beginning to feel overwhelmed. Desperately she pushed it back down and tried to keep calm. Another deep breath. Time for a test.

"What is your name?" she asked, but not spoken aloud this time, just in her head. There was no answer. It might claim to be inside her but it seemed only verbal communication was possible. Did that mean it was real and she wasn't hallucinating, or can hallucinations only hear when you talk out loud? She had no idea.

"What do you want with me?" she asked, out loud this time.

"I want you to save the world."

The overwhelming panic was back in force. A dark river splashing against her chest, getting ever harder to resist. "You mean you want me to go on some crusade to save people's souls?"

"No. I want you to find a way to prevent the Earth's destruction and the obliteration of the human race."

The dark waters were lapping at her throat, her breaths now shallow, fluttering gasps. She tried as best she could to keep calm.

"And if I somehow save the planet from whatever problem it's got will you leave me alone and let me go home?"

"You can never go home."

The river was rising up to engulf her, she was only holding on by a thread as she asked her last question.

"So what happens to me afterwards?"

The answer was so devastating all hope of self control was lost. Floundering, lost and broken she was no longer able to keep her head above the dark, overwhelming waters of panic and despair.

7

A Strange Place

For a long time the universe remained a strange place. For the first 380,000 years it was foggy almost to the point of being opaque. Photons of light were being quickly absorbed and scattered by free roaming electrons.

Even after the universe became transparent it was still pitch black because there were no stars. It was another 150 million years before the first star shone alone in the darkness. Both the matter and anti-matter halves of the universe went through the same evolution.

Throughout the expansion the entities quietly existed, observing and where necessary adapting. They watched tiny chemical reactions happening over fractions of a second and stars swirling into galaxies over billions of years. They had no sense of boredom or impatience. In fact they had no feelings at all. They were creatures of unfeeling logic. Despite their great intelligence and power their objectives were simple, unchanged from their primitive origins. Growth was no longer possible but the urge to exist and explore their surroundings remained. So when the first stars brought new light into the darkness they readied themselves to move and investigate.

In the inner regions where matter was abundant these creatures of anti-matter had to tread carefully. They could store matter and perform simple manipulations upon it provided it was kept a safe distance from their own bodies. So they held clumps of it as a fuel source, expending it and precious parts of their own anti-matter bodies to generate the power needed to move.

They moved at around half the speed of light because as speed increases the power required goes up exponentially and above that speed it becomes prohibitive. While moving they reshaped themselves into a long stream, actively repelled everything around them and pushed a clump of matter ahead of them the size of a small moon to act as a shield.

As the galaxies formed they all set out to explore the stars and planets. Even at half of the speed of light there are so many stars in a galaxy that it was going to take hundreds of billions of years to explore just one, not that they were in a hurry.

In the galaxy where humans were destined to evolve only two entities were stranded and they were fortunate enough to meet after just 5 billion years. Before parting they exchanged quantum entangled particles so they would be able to continue communicating over any distance. It was rather more unfortunate when, 13.8 billion years after the creation of the universe, one of them stumbled across the Earth.

8

Choose Again

"Not that it wasn't a blast, but I thought we were done," said the Old Man.

"It's the girl. It's not working out. I think you should choose again."

"I'm surprised to hear that, she struck me as eminently suitable. How long have you been together?"

"Two minutes thirty five seconds from first contact."

"You blew it in two minutes thirty five seconds? Did you listen to *any* of my advice?"

"I brought her to a tranquil place."

"Not so tranquil now I suspect." He was looking at the indentation in the grass where the girl must have been lying. Much of the grass around where her arms would have been had been hammered with some force, the rest had been ripped out and thrown around. "Surely you didn't blurt out she had to save the planet in the first two minutes?"

"She asked what I wanted from her."

He rolled his eyes skyward. "Osiris give me strength. You'll just have to try to calm her."

"Communication has become impossible. Whenever I try to contact

30

her she covers her ears with her hands and shouts 'la la la-la lah' at the top of her voice."

He took a sip from the glass of cool mineral water his friend had obligingly given to him while he tried to suppress a smile. "And this behaviour started after you told her she had to save the planet?" he asked, and took a deeper drink.

"No. After I told her that if she succeeds she would have fulfilled her mission and I would then be able to terminate her existence."

Water exploded from the Old Man's mouth and nose.

"You told her WHAT?!"

9

Earth

The entity had found organic life before, but it was rare and had never progressed beyond single celled organisms. The Earth of 2702 B.C. was a very different place where life had evolved far beyond those primitive beginnings. It called its twin brother who immediately changed course to Earth.

While waiting for its arrival the entity cast repeated sensor nets over the Earth below and attempted to ascertain the objectives and thought processes of the creatures that inhabited it, particularly of the humans.

Universal Chaos was a concept it was familiar with. Some things in the universe, particularly at a particle level, can simply never be known with certainty, probability is the best you can do. Here, however, were whole brains acting in an apparently chaotic fashion. In the same set of circumstances one individual would choose one action and another individual a different one. It watched in puzzlement at a host of mysteries. A hungry woman who chose to skip meals, a man and woman who formed a good match but then chose not to reproduce, a child trying to take a toy from another even though it did not want it.

This 'Organic Chaos' appeared to make no sense when looking at individuals but when seen as a whole, as if the entire species were a single organism, it was successful, growing and learning.

It took just 146 years for its brother to arrive as it had not been far away. It too cast sensor nets on the Earth and then spoke.

"Thank you for showing me this, I would not have wanted to miss it. Are you ready to destroy them now?"

The first was as surprised as it is possible for a creature with no emotions to be. *"We are clones. How is it possible for us to look at the same planet and arrive at such different conclusions? I see it as a valuable resource to study Organic Chaos. I feel we can learn more by studying them than we can from exploring thousands of stars."*

"I disagree. They have a drive to learn and while the humans are unfocused and divided if they were to ever work in unison their combined intelligence would rival our own and their creativity would exceed it. Technology is progressing and I predict it will progress at an escalating rate. If we leave now it may be another billion years before we meet them again but by then it is inevitable they will have discovered powerful weapons of mass destruction, inevitable that they will eventually discover our presence, and inevitable that at some point they will decide to use them on us. It is the inherent danger of an emotional rather than logical organism."

"That was not my conclusion."

"Nevertheless it is mine, and I must act in the interests of us both."

With those words it formed an antimatter cluster, detached it from its body, shielded it and fired it at the Earth. The small container dropped through the atmosphere leaving a trail of fire and smoke before being extinguished in the Pacific Ocean with a towering fountain at its point of impact. It sank quickly a full 11 kilometres into the pitch black waters of the Marianas Trench, the deepest place on the planet. Once it had reached the bottom the newcomer said, *"Keep a safe distance, brother,"* and dissolved the shield. At least that is what it tried to do, only to discover his twin blocking him and preventing the anti-matter release.

Quickly both sides flashed through all the possible offensive and defensive options. Even if they had wanted to a direct attack on the other would have resulted in a stalemate. On Earth neither could so much as move a grain of sand without the other blocking it, let alone take any offensive action.

Despite the impasse neither side was prepared to back down. There was no animosity but both shared a rigid determination that their view was correct and must prevail. There was no need for communication for all the facts were known, as were the strategies both must follow.

It's brother switched to patient, indirect influence and manipulation of the very beings it was trying to destroy. It was glacially slow but time was of no consequence to either being. Chess pieces would be moved by highly intelligent beings on a field of play of which they both had only a shaky understanding.

So for more than four millennia the secret war was fought. At first opportunities were few and the defending entity easily prevailed, but as time and technology moved on it became harder and harder to foil the attacks. Now the most ambitious offensive of all had been launched and the defending entity was completely oblivious.

10

The Mission

The entity dissolved the Old Man and restored Alex to her dip in the grass. It then stayed silent as the Old Man had told it to. Alex sobbed quietly and then screamed at it that she wanted to go home, before returning to sobbing. It was a pattern that repeated several times until finally there were no more tears ready to fall. Still the entity waited another ten minutes before finally saying, *"I'm not going to harm you."*

"That's not what you said a moment ago. You said you were going to kill me," she accused.

"Since then I consulted with the Old Man who pointed out the error of my ways, or as he put it 'Of all the stupid, crass, insensitive and plain idiotic things I have heard in my long life that one is the dooziest ever. It must have taken you centuries to think of an idea that dumb'. Actually there was a lot more of it and I'm still not sure what the word 'dooziest' means but I got the idea he disapproved."

Alex could not help smiling despite herself. "He's right. Whatever you do don't get a job designing employee incentive schemes or the workers will have all topped themselves by lunchtime. I think I'd like to meet him again, we may have a lot in common."

"Sadly that is unlikely, for reasons I will explain later. Next I should tell you that the Old Man has suggested an idea for a reward if you succeed in permanently securing the safety of the planet, an idea I have accepted. It is..."

"Whoa! Stop there", said Alex. "Let's just leave it that you won't kill me and it will be a nice surprise." She had an unpleasant feeling that it would still not involve returning to her family but she would rather live with the hope than have it dashed.

"Very well. Then I will just say it is a good prize which would be the envy of your race."

"That sounds good - but no more clues OK?"

"OK"

Alex took three long, slow deep breaths during which neither side spoke. Finally Alex was ready to ask the question. "So what's this job you've got for me?"

"There are two large, powerful alien entities near the Earth. One is myself and the other is my identical twin brother. We are almost as old as the universe, just a split second younger."

"So far, so crazy. Just pretend I'm believing this for now and I'll do the same."

That wasn't the response it had hoped for, but it supposed anything was an improvement on 'la la la'.

"My brother has come to the conclusion that your race is a threat and should be destroyed, whereas I feel we can learn from you and have so far blocked all his attempts to act against you. We are perfectly matched."

"I don't see where I come in."

"My brother uses an agent; a human protected from me who acts on his behalf. His agent tries to manipulate events to bring about a

mass extinction. Whenever he has an agent I can use some of my energy to have an agent of my own. When he has none I must hold that energy in reserve, otherwise he could attack the planet directly and overwhelm me."

"And if he used two agents...?"

"Then I could do the same, but he never has. Indeed for thousands of years he rarely had any, but since weapons of mass destruction have been invented he is almost constantly at work trying to trigger their use. He also has a longer term strategy which has met with some success in preventing humans taking any action to prevent Global Warming. However his actions are not always so clear. His agents have learnt to be cunning. They know I am watching them just as he is watching you now."

Alex felt distinctly uncomfortable at the thought. She felt a prickling sensation and hairs rising on the back of her neck.

"They frequently obscure their actions or lay false trails. One of your main tasks is to help me understand what he is attempting. Right now, for example, he is working hard to get a temple built. It seems quite inexplicable. Maybe it is a diversion. Once we have ascertained his purpose your job is to find a way to stop him."

"I can't do all that, I'm just a kid. Choose somebody else."

"The Old Man chose you. He felt your youth provides you with a valuable flexibility of thought, and your courage impressed him."

"Who is this old man anyway?"

"Your predecessor. He retired and chose you to replace him. He felt his own knowledge of Earth was dangerously out of date - a shame as I have always valued his counsel. He told me you would find the task daunting. Despite the inaccuracy of the statement he said I should tell you that you have certain 'super powers' to aid you."

"I do?" said Alex, unable to hide the sudden interest in her voice. "What super powers would those be?" she asked, trying and failing to sound blasé.

"I can perform actions that affect your body, but nothing beyond it as those would be blocked. For example I can move you anywhere on the planet in a matter of seconds, it will seem instantaneous to you."

"So if I wanted to stand on Ayres Rock do I tap my heels three times and wish for…" She didn't finish her sentence because the meadow dissolved and was replaced with a scene that was like its negative. Pale moonlight replaced warm sunlight, the hard rock of Uluru replaced soft grass, the cold air of a desert night replaced the warm air of the meadow, and the flat fields around her became rocky drops curving down to a barren desert floor far below, given a ghostly appearance by the almost full moon.

"Take me back," she gasped and the meadow returned. Suddenly she knew in her heart this was all very real. "A-anything else?" she asked a little more tentatively.

"You are invulnerable."

"Very, very cool," she said, mulling over the possibilities it opened up.

"And you can learn new languages, though it will cause headaches."

"Always did at school."

"Almost anything else is possible within the confines of your body. The Old Man experimented with turning his surface into a three dimensional hologram upon which images could be displayed. He was fond of it but it never proved particularly useful."

"Oh I don't know about that. I'll be able to sit in front of a mirror and watch movies."

"The enemy agents have the same abilities, of course."

"Oh." There was a long pause. "You know, I guess I can help you out though I'm still not sure how much help a 14 year old is going to be to you with or without super powers, but first

I really have to get back to my parents. Just for a while, they must be worried sick. So if you could just teleport me home we can meet up later and save the world, say 9am tomorrow morning?"

"No"

"What do you mean 'No'?"

"*I mean you can not visit your parents and you are not 14 years old.*"

"Don't go losing your marbles on me. I think I know how old I am and why won't you let me go back, am I a prisoner?"

"*Because you are not Alex. You were created just over an hour ago. You are a molecule by molecule copy of Alex created out of material linked to my own body. The real Alex was taken to hospital for a check-up and even now is being released into the care of her parents who drove to the hospital to pick her up. You may want to choose a new name.*"

11

Ralph

The gun on Ralph's hip was uncomfortable. It was heavy and awkward when walking, and made the skin underneath sweat. He had tried to tell them he didn't need it but they were insistent. The situation outside the temple perimeter's barbed wire fences was volatile and they lived in the constant and very real fear of armed attack. Not Ralph of course, but he could hardly tell them that God had made him invulnerable.

He was standing in one of the more complete rooms, not that it looked it because it was being used for mixed storage. Building materials were heaped against the walls and on a floor turned white by cement dust there were scattered scaffolding joints which made walking something that had to be done with care. Near the corner furthest from the open doorway sat a battered desk in a relatively clear patch, though no chair. Bending over the architect's drawings covering the desk Ralph tried to work out if they could make do with a reduced tile shipment following the ambush of a supply truck. Maybe he could thin out the higher tiles to make patterns rather than the planned continuous wall. No, if this was worth doing it was worth doing properly. And it was more than worth doing - it was an honour, no matter how arduous. He would just have to reorder and guard the truck better this time.

"Hello," said a voice, making Ralph jump. He spun round to see a young girl. How had security been so lax as to allow an outsider to stroll all the way into his office at the heart of the complex?

"Beware. She is an agent of the enemy," said the archangel in his ear.

Grabbing his crucifix he held it up and with blazing eyes commanded, "I banish thee, spawn of Satan. In the name of the Lord leave this holy place of worship."

"Spawn of Satan, eh? My brother called me that once. Mind you I had just accidentally wiped out all his PlayStation save games. I'm still not sure how I did it. My name's Alex by the way. My side wants me to change it but I think it's a pretty name. What do you think?"

"Er... it's nice enough, I suppose," he said, rather nonplussed, then added quickly, "for a creature of darkness."

"I gather the original Ralph died in a gas explosion. Suspicious circumstances and all that. You must feel a bit put out that your own side killed you. You do *know* you're just a copy, don't you?"

"I have no idea what you're talking about," replied Ralph. God had saved him from the explosion, though thinking about it there was that mysterious body in the ruins. No, the girl was just trying to sow the seeds of doubt and confusion as do all Satan's creatures.

"You're just over 19 months old. As for me - I'm one week old today, so I'm thinking of having a birthday cake to celebrate. Yes, I think that would be an excellent idea. If you don't mind?"

41

The last was not directed at Ralph but somewhere in the middle distance. A fairy cake appeared in her hand with icing on top and a single lit candle.

"Hmm... A bit on the small side but it looks tasty enough. Would you like a bite?" A distracted look came over her for a moment followed by, "Oh, sorry, apparently you can't. It would involve giving body mass from one entity to another and that's not the done thing. Pity. You're American aren't you?"

The constant switches in conversation were bewildering but he was determined not to be bested. "Yes, that's right, and your accent sounds British. Home Counties English if I'm not mistaken".

"O bravo. I was on holiday once when some Americans asked me if I was Australian. You can't get any more wrong than that without falling off the planet, but you're right on the button."

"I studied at Cambridge for a year on a college exchange."

"Did you? How impressive. What were you studying?"

"Architecture."

"Ah yes, of course. That and some string pulling is how you got the temple building job. Did I tell you my name was Alex? I think I did. Did you know the Old Man never chose a new name? He said he was waiting for the right one to occur to him and it never did. That's why we just call him the Old Man. It's hopelessly unoriginal. My name is short for Alexis which means 'Defender'. Rather appropriate with people like you about, isn't it?"

"Not really, your side is the one people need to be protected against," he insisted.

"I guess it depends on your point of view. Do you speak Hebrew, Ralph? Seeing as how you are building a temple in Israel I can see how that would be useful. Learning languages is one of my super powers so I guess you must be able to do it too."

"It's not a 'super power', it's a miracle granted by God."

"Whatever. Did it give you a headache? It did me, and some weird confusion for a few days."

"It was a small price to pay for a great gift."

"Do you know why? My entity - you know I'm going to have to think of a name for you - how about Bob?" A pause. "Well I don't care what you think. It's Bob until one of us thinks of something better. Where was I? Oh yes. Bob says he has to find somebody who speaks both English and Hebrew whose language centre in the brain is exactly the same size as mine, and then he overwrites mine with a copy of theirs. Sounds a bit scary to me but he assures me he can change it back any time. The headaches are due to all the loose ends; neurons that don't match up or some such, but a good night's sleep sorts out most of those. The confusion is because words often trigger memories, but the memories aren't there - they are in someone else's head."

"I suppose that makes sense," said Ralph warily but walking into her trap all the same.

"But of course if your language ability was given to you by God there shouldn't be any loose ends or headaches should there? Or does God make mistakes?"

"God is perfect," he replied, not even attempting to answer the conundrum.

"I always thought so, which proves beyond all reasonable doubt that she's female."

Ralph was at a loss what to say so Alex kept the pressure up by firing another question at him. "So what are you up to today?"

"I'm building a temple, obviously," replied Ralph with more

firmness in his voice, wondering how he was ever going to gain the initiative.

"Why?"

"Because it was p…"

"Silence. She is keeping you off balance and you are in danger of giving much away."

"It was 'P'? It was purple? It was pleasant? It was pretty pointless?"

Ralph kept his lips sealed, so Alex changed tack yet again.

"Did you know your 'evil one' arrived here in 2556 BC, but his first attempt to wipe out the human race wasn't until the 17th century? There just weren't that many opportunities in those days." She had watched Ralph to see if the 'evil one' jibe would unseal his lips but they just compressed tighter into two thin, white lines.

"He got his little helper to travel round Europe with a cage full of black plague infested rats, releasing them one at a time in major population centres. It drove the Old Man to distraction trying to stop him. A lightning bolt in each rat would have been best but of course your entity - let's call him Lucifer…"

Ralph opened his mouth to say something then forced it shut again.

"… would have blocked it. The poor guy was reduced to following him round with a cage full of hungry cats. I'm afraid it didn't work very well, though the plague didn't turn out to be as deadly as your guy had hoped either.

"You know it must be tough being Lucifer. It must be hard to get people to do what you want if you can't tell them the truth. You can't just clone some guy and say 'I want you to help me exterminate the human race, how about it?' So how did he get you on board - 40 pieces of silver?"

Ralph could not contain himself any longer. 'By promising death and eternal suffering for evil doers like you".

"SILENCE"

"While the deserving will be granted r…" began Ralph but then turned into transparent smoke and vanished.

"Roses?" called Alex after him. "Ravioli?" But he was gone.

"You have quite a talent for annoying people."

"Thanks, my brother always said the same."

"Twice then I think he was on the verge of saying too much. If you can figure out what, it may help."

"So now you think I might be the one for the job?"

"You know, I think you might."

12

The Beach

When people look for the perfect beach they look for clean white sand, hot dry sun and a sky whose bright blue colour is bettered only by the pale blue beauty of a crystal clear sea. But to really make it onto the world's top ten it needs some extra features which don't spring to mind so readily.

People think they want a deserted beach to themselves but after an hour of roasting they start to look round for a hammock in the shade of a palm tree and a place to buy an ice laden cocktail.

If bars and cafes are present there should only be a couple, well spaced out. They must be made with uneven wooden poles, topped with a palm thatched roof of dubious benefit if it ever rained and run by a lively, friendly character. Perhaps one with dreadlocks and a Bob Marley T-shirt who looks so laid back he's ready to fall off his chair but somehow manages to effortlessly rustle up excellent Margaritas.

Then there are the palm trees. A line of palm trees are essential, of course, but what people forget is that at least one of them needs to lean sharply towards the sea. If the angle at the base is shallow enough angle women will rush to lie on the jagged bark of the trunk, trying desperately to look relaxed and comfortable on its rough surface just long enough for a companion to take a photograph.

This beach had all that and more. Two simple outrigger boats lay upturned on the beach with small fishing nets tucked underneath. The bright primary red and yellow paint on their hulls had only just started to chip and peel, adding the final missing colours to the scene.

The leaning palm had something else that particularly appealed to Alex - a knotted rope hung down from near the top, reaching down almost to the water. She grabbed hold of it and ran out of the sea with a jewelled fan of water spraying up in front of her. She ran up the beach and the rope length was just long enough for her to reach the base of a second tree with a short ladder fastened to its trunk. Eagerly she scrambled up to a platform just big enough for one. She paused for a moment, both hands gripping the rope directly above one of the knots. Then with a whoop she launched herself off, clamping her feet to the rope above the lowest knot.

She arced over the water then, before it reached the furthest point as it was still climbing skywards, she let go with her hands and used her legs to propel herself as high as possible into the air. An excited, exhilarated yell cut through the peaceful beach as she shot both high and long before her voice was cut off abruptly with a big splash from her less-than-graceful entry into the sea. She surfaced, spluttering from some of the water that had gone up her nose but laughing too.

Swimming to the shore she suddenly dived under and then asked Bob a question in a flurry of bubbles.

"I didn't catch that."

Her head popped back to the surface, laughing again. "So I can hear you underwater but you can't hear me?"

"You can hear me because I vibrate your ear drums to match the sounds I want you to hear. I can't read your thoughts so you must speak out loud for me to hear. You should also bear in mind that the enemy can hear your voice, though not mine."

"Hello, Lucifer," she said cheerfully, giving a little wave as she stood up and walked out of the water onto the beach.

"You don't seem to be taking this seriously."

"Oh I am", she countered. "In fact I've been thinking about Ralph's unfinished sentences. I think maybe the first word was 'planned', as in 'It was planned a long time ago'. It could also be 'paid for' and he was about to tell us who by."

"Maybe. I don't see how that helps us."

"Give me time. I'll figure it out, I'm sure a rest will help."

She walked back to the line of palms, strolling slowly at first then getting gradually faster as the hot sand began to burn her feet. By the time she reached the shade and collapsed into a hammock she was dancing from foot to foot.

"What an ace place. So much better than all the others. Can I have an orange juice and lemonade please, with bucket loads of ice." Followed by, "Ice in the drink I meant". Two buckets filled to the brim with ice promptly disappeared again.

Once she had finished squirming and was satisfied the hammock was as comfortable and stable as possible she asked, "Why do you use agents that are copies of real humans? Why not just make a human looking shell and get it to do whatever you want?"

"We have no emotions therefore an artificial human would be as unconvincing as a robot. We would have little idea how to make it react to stimuli. A cloned human agent also brings extra benefits.

Although we are highly intelligent we are not particularly creative. We are good at solving problems of logic but poor at thinking of unconventional solutions. You have a great deal more chance of discovering what the opposition is up to than me, for all my power and intelligence."

"Tell me, have you ever come close to losing? I mean the human race nearly going kabooey?"

"Twice, and curiously neither was due to the opposition."

"Ooh. Do tell," she said, sitting up slightly to listen, though it made no difference to the clarity of his voice.

"The first was in the early 1960s. I had become concerned that the West had a large number of nuclear weapons capable of striking Russia. If you include aircraft-launched bombs America had eight times more nuclear weapons than Russia. On land Russia had only 20 vulnerable surface launched missiles whereas America had 180 in hardened silos plus more stationed in Britain, Italy and Turkey. At sea America had 144 long range Polaris missiles in submarines, whereas Russia had only 100 short range missiles in submarines so primitive they could only fire on the surface where they would be extremely vulnerable. Submarines NATO was skilled at tracking.

"Worst of all a spy had described all Russia's military weakness in great detail. I was very worried that America might feel it could seize the opportunity to win a nuclear war, and there were some who were advising just that.

"Using a Russian agent I managed to persuade the Russian leader, Khrushchev, that it was vital he create a credible deterrent to close this window of opportunity. I believed that no rational country would launch nuclear weapons if they knew they would be wiped out by the response, a policy that later became known as 'Mutually Assured Destruction', or simply MAD.

"I pointed out that Cuba would make an excellent missile base.

The short range meant the existing rather dated Russian technology would be perfectly adequate. I saw the chance to secure peace.

"Unfortunately the Americans spotted the start of the operation and it triggered the Cuban Missile Crisis. The closest the world has ever come to nuclear war, and entirely of my own doing."

"Oops. Well we all make mistakes. Don't beat yourself up about it."

"There is little room for mistakes. I have only to fail once and all is lost."

"What about the second time?"

"It is right now."

"What!? Did I miss something? Did Ralph just kick over a canister of bio-weapons or something?"

"No, nothing like that. I am wondering whether to keep fighting. I am increasingly of the opinion that I am wrong and my brother is right. The human race should be destroyed."

Alex held her hands up in the shape of the letter T. "Whoa there. Whoa, whoa, timeout, pause, hold everything. I thought I had my work cut out trying to stop your brother and now you say I have to stop you too?"

"Yes"

"What's the problem? Why the change of heart?"

"When I first arrived I believed you humans had something I named 'organic chaos' - a fascinating randomness to your decision making which I was keen to preserve and study."

"And now?"

"Now I think I was mistaken. Every action a human takes is for a reason. Some of those reasons are hard to understand, they may be unconscious motivations and heavily influenced by emotions, but even emotions are born of rational objectives."

"So everything I do makes sense?" she said sticking her

tongue out and waving a leg in the air making her continued presence in the hammock tenuous at best.

"Far from it, but it is rational," adding, *"however hard it is sometimes to fathom the reason,"* because Alex seemed to have got distracted and was testing whether it was possible to get her foot in her ear. *"All of your major psychologists agree."*

"So if it's all doom and gloom why haven't you turned the Earth into dust yet, what are you waiting for?" she asked, then suddenly had an empty feeling in the pit of her stomach in case her words were all it took to set him off on a killing spree.

"In case there is a God."

"Huh?"

"I do not believe there is a God, however it is a major theme on Earth. I would like to be sure before doing anything irreversible and losing my only source of research. Furthermore I would prefer not to take any action that might incur the wrath of a more powerful being. So I am giving you an opportunity to persuade me."

"So you not only want me to stop a super-powerful psychopathic alien, but now you want me to persuade you God exists? And if I fail doing either one the planet blows up?"

"Yes. The Old Man felt out of his depth on religion, that more than anything prompted his retirement."

"Can't say I know much about it either. Maybe we should go and see a priest." She looked thoughtful for a moment then tried to leap up exclaiming, "It's not..." but the hammock spun her round and spat her out into the sand. Ignoring the undignified exit she bounced back to her feet and said excitedly, "It's not 'planning' or 'paid for', Ralph was about to say 'It was prophesied'. Now we definitely have to talk to a priest."

"Of all the humans I have met you come the closest to organic chaos."

"Thanks. I think."

13

Tom

The priest was dripping. He had no idea how such a small child with tiny flailing arms had managed to scoop that much water out of the font. In fact he had no idea there had even been that much water to start with. There was certainly a lot less now. Fortunately they had all finally left and no more soggy handshakes were required at the church door, no more polite declining of invitations to their 'small celebration'. All he wanted to do was get to the vestry and change out of his wet robes.

"Hello," said a voice beside him, "I'm Alex".

A girl was sitting in one of the forward pews.

"Hello," he replied, rather startled that he had not seen her come in. "I'm Tom."

"Father Tom?"

"No, I'm not keen on all that high church stuff, plain Tom is all. If you insist on a title then 'Vicar' will do, though technically I am 'Chaplain to the Isles'."

"Why are you all wet?"

"I just had a baptism."

"I thought you would have been christened long ago, what with you being a priest."

"I was. I meant I was conducting a baptism for a baby."

"Oh, I hope you saved it some of the water."

"Was there something I can help you with?" he asked with an inaudible sigh.

"Yes, two things. The first one is I want to prove to my friend that God exists otherwise a lot of people might get hurt."

The vicar wondered whether it was Wednesday, for some reason Wednesdays were always a trial. It was not.

"Tell you what, I'll just change out of my wet things, then we can have a chat over a cup of tea in the vestry. How about that?"

"Sounds good to me."

Ten minutes later they were sitting in a cosy but cluttered room. It doubled as an overflow storage area with many of the choir's cassocks hanging on a rack along one side while a wall of hymn books encroached from another.

Tom and Alex sat at right angles on creaky chairs, the floral pattern on the unevenly padded seats almost too faded to make out.

In their hands they held mismatched mugs of steaming tea, and on the wobbly coffee table in front of them was a bowl of chocolate chip biscuits to which Alex had just helped herself eagerly.

"Yes I am," she said to nobody in particular. "Well you can just leave behind all the 'foreign molecules' when I go. Chocolate chip cookies are my favourite."

"I beg your pardon?" said Tom, suddenly worried that the girl might not be entirely sane.

"Oh, sorry, it's just my invisible friend. Don't mind him."

"Um… OK," said Tom, double checking it was not Wednesday.

Then, deciding it was time to get the conversation onto familiar territory stated more than asked, "So you want to know whether God exists."

"Yes please."

"Naturally I am going to say yes as I've devoted my entire life to him, but I'm afraid there can never be any proof, just pointers, otherwise there is no room for faith."

"Are the pointers really, really convincing?"

"Not in the way you hope. In the end you have to make that leap of faith to believe in God. It wouldn't be the same if I gave you his telephone number."

"That's a shame, it's going to make things difficult. My friend says the fact there are hundreds of religions with conflicting beliefs weakens the case for God. If there was a 'Universal Truth' shouldn't it be more obvious?"

It was not the first time somebody had talked to him about the religious interest of a mythical 'friend', and if she wanted to talk about it in the third person rather than admit her own interest that was fine by him.

"There is another way of looking at it. In my view none of us has got it right yet, but perhaps all of the religions have uncovered different parts of the truth. Somebody described God as a sea washing onto a shore. You would get a very different view of the sea depending where you stood. You might see a rocky cove with waves spraying over it, a blowhole spouting water up from a part submerged cave, a quiet fjord or a peaceful beach. In the end, though, they are all just different faces of the same ocean. In the same way we have many faiths with different views but they are all different views of the same God.

"Here's another thought for you. You say there are hundreds

of religions, I'd say thousands if you look back in history. They have existed as long as mankind has - but is that a reason to doubt God or confirm your faith? For tens of thousands of years across the globe one thing has held constant, an inbuilt feeling in all mankind that there is a being greater than they. If you want a strong pointer to the existence of God I can think of none better than an inherent need in his people."

"He makes some good points. I will consider this further."

"Thanks, that was just what I needed. My other question is about Temple Mount in Jerusalem. Is there some prophesy about a temple there?"

"Hmm... not in the conventional Church, but I heard the End Timers think there is."

"End Timers?" she queried with interest. "Who are they?"

"An extremist and surprisingly influential Christian group who believe the Second Coming of Christ is about to happen and with it the end of the world."

"Really?" said Alex, very interested now. "Can you tell me more?"

"I'm afraid not. It's not a subject I know much about. You don't live anywhere near Oxford do you?"

"It's on my way home," she replied. After all, everywhere could be on her way home.

"I have a friend there, a professor in the Faculty of Theology. He's an expert on modern world religions and the End Timers are one of his particular interests. He's a lovely fellow and enjoys chatting to enthusiastic students. I've got his card here somewhere."

Finding the card took longer than expected in the vestry clutter but eventually it came to light in the back of a battered address book beneath the overflow cassocks.

"I'll give him a call and let him know you are coming. He's back at University now but I don't think lectures have started yet."

"Oh, no need," said Alex, "as I'm not sure when it will be. Must run, thanks for the tea and biscuits, you've been a great help." Then she was sprinting for the door clutching the professor's card.

Bit of a wildcat that one, Tom thought to himself. I'd better phone and warn him she's on the way.

After checking his newly rediscovered address book he picked up the phone and dialled.

"Hello, it's Tom... yes you remember right, I'm in the Isles of Scilly now - Chaplain to the Isles. Still settling in but it's been going well and of course it's a beautiful place... Listen, I was just talking to girl called Alex who is very interested in the End Timers so I suggested she stop by and speak to you... What? Oh, er... brown hair, brown eyes, 13-15 years old, quite pretty, freckles, full of energy and wearing a Wonder Woman T-shirt when I saw her... no, she can't be, she left not two minutes ago."

"Well she is," said the voice on the telephone. "She's sitting in my office right now."

14

Professor Dalton

Alex stopped swinging her legs under the oak table on which she had perched and put her hand in front of her 'O' shaped mouth.

She was in the office of Professor Richard Dalton. He was a well respected figure in the department and had been assigned one of the bigger rooms. The dark oak floor and furniture in no way made the room look gloomy, just old and venerable. Everything was built to last. It had served many past occupants and would undoubtedly last long enough to serve many more. Much of the furniture consisted of glass fronted book cases which lined two of the walls, but even they could not contain the prolific numbers of books, so more were stacked on and around the desk Alex was sitting on.

Two large windows let in plenty of light, in front of one of which was a seating area with three faded leather chairs set around a low table. From there the nearby fifteenth century Divinity School could be glimpsed. All the University buildings radiated a feeling of age, continuity and prestige to a greater or lesser extent, but as one of the first buildings at Oxford built for one of the oldest faculties the feeling near that one was almost palpable.

Professor Dalton was standing with the phone in his hand twisting round and looking piercingly at Alex. A voice at the other end reminded him he was still connected. He said something about calling him back and put the receiver down, still staring. Alex took the hand away from her mouth and said, "Was that Tom by any chance?"

"Yes"

"Oops!"

"Would you care to explain how you can be in the Isles of Scilly one moment and Oxford the next?"

"No… er yes. I have a twin sister, she looks exactly like me. You'd think we were clones."

"And was that her speaking to Tom?"

An interplay of conflicting emotions played across her face. It was plain as day she was deciding whether to lie. Finally she looked resigned and said, "No".

"You were wondering whether to lie, why didn't you?"

"I thought lying to a priest was probably a sin."

"Unlike many of my colleagues I am not ordained, I'm just a professor, a school teacher if you prefer."

"Really? In that case it was my twin sister."

"You're not very good at lying are you?"

"My English teacher says that's my one redeeming feature. Can I have a cup of tea please, and do you have any chocolate chip biscuits?"

"Tea I can manage, indeed the kettle has just boiled and right now I feel very much in need of a cup myself."

He walked over to a small cabinet and made a pot of Twinings English Breakfast Tea. Putting the pot, two smart tea cups and some biscuits on a tray he carried them carefully over to the table. Alex followed and took a seat.

"Now, are you going to tell me what's going on?" he asked as he poured out the tea.

"These are Ginger Nuts," she said making a face. "Tom had Chocolate Chip. I bet he gets heaps more visitors than you. I heard a bit of what he was saying. I think he said I was pretty. Did he say I was pretty?"

"Are you trying to change the subject?"

"Yes. Is it working?"

"No"

There was silence for a moment while Alex dunked her biscuit in her tea for longer than was wise until, predictably, a chunk broke off. It fell as a soggy lump to the bottom of the cup to her consternation.

"So are you going to tell me how you got here?" he prompted again.

"No, sorry. I can't."

"And yet you expect me to help you?"

"Yes, I suppose that's not very fair is it? Well... what if I just said I've got super powers, like Wonder Woman," she said pointing to her T-shirt, "and super heroes don't go round explaining how it works to everyone they meet or they would never get anything done, would they?"

"I suppose not. Do you have a lot of 'powers'?"

"Not that many really. I can only do things that affect my body, nothing outside it because that would get blocked."

"What by?"

"That's a long story and I'm definitely not allowed to tell you about that."

"Are you worried I'll tell what I know so far?"

"No, not really. They'll just say, 'That poor Mr. Dalton, he cracked after taking 6B for Religious Studies' and somebody else will say 'I can't blame him, I feel like screaming every time I take 6B. Poor bloke. I heard they took him away in a padded ambulance.'"

Professor Dalton smiled. "There is no class 6B but I take your point. Maybe you should tell me what you came here for."

Alex was relieved to be off the spot. "I want to know about the End Timers and why they want to build a temple on Temple Mount in Jerusalem."

"Ah, one of my particular interests as it happens. In fact I recently returned from a research trip to America to find out more. I'm afraid I was er… thrown out of one of their meetings."

"Cool. What for?"

"I'm embarrassed to say that for a moment I lost my objectivity. Something a speaker said hit a nerve and I got up on stage and said exactly what I thought which was highly unprofessional. Not surprisingly it didn't go down well. I can't think what came over me." He looked as uncomfortable as Alex had a moment ago and quickly moved on.

"Briefly, they believe many prophesies concerning the end of the world have now been fulfilled and once the rest have come to pass everything ends. Some even think it is overdue and are keen to help it along."

"Why would they do that?"

"Because they look forward to the Second Coming of Christ. They think the world will suffer seven years of tribulation before the final end, but all the righteous can skip that as they will be 'raptured' - meaning they will be whisked away to meet God. Actually there is a lot of debate among them as to which prophesies are left to fulfil and the sequence they…"

"Rapture!" Alex burst out. "That's what the 'R' word is!" Then in answer to the professor's puzzled look, "One of the er... enemy. Super heroes always have super enemies, you know. He promised that evil doers like me would have eternal suffering, but the deserving would be granted rapture, only he never managed to get the last word out."

"I expect somebody interrupted him," he said wryly.

"Oops. Sorry, I interrupted you, didn't I?" she said looking abashed.

"No problem. I was going to say the belief is based on very shaky foundations. For example the word 'Rapture' does not appear anywhere in the bible. It was probably first invented in 1830 by a 15 year old girl in Scotland who said she had a vision, which seems a weak starting point on which to build such an enormous belief structure. Advocates dip into the bible for supporting passages, but they tend to pick and choose their text and stretch interpretations to the breaking point. For example much of the apocalyptic language clearly refers to the end of the Roman Empire which is awkward since the last remnants of the empire died out over 500 years ago. Those that concede the point get round it by saying the European Union is a revived Roman Empire!"

"What about the temple?" prompted Alex, before the conversation became too scholarly.

"Ah yes. There are certain prerequisites before it all kicks off, so to speak. The biggest one is the building of the third Jewish temple on Temple Mount. For years that has been a major problem because after the first two temples were destroyed the Muslims came along and found the mount in ruins and being used as a rubbish tip so they built a mosque there, the 'Dome of the Rock' and later declared this was the point at which Muhammad had ascended into heaven. That makes it the third most holy place in the world to them, surpassed only by Mecca and Medina, which is awkward as it is also the Jews holiest site.

"Some extreme Jews have tried to take action in the past. In 1961 an Australian tried to burn the Dome down, followed by an armed raid in 1983 and a bomb attempt in 1984 which were both foiled, the latter apparently funded by End Timers. Then in 1990 a group called the 'Temple Mount Faithful' were reported to be trying to lay a symbolic foundation stone of a new Jewish temple at the site. In the riots that followed seventeen people died. After that the group were prevented from returning though they often tried. Instead they took to drawing up plans and creating all the contents ready for a future building.

"The big news, however, was two years ago. The region has always been prone to earthquakes and around a third of the Dome of the Rock collapsed following a big one, leaving the other two thirds much weakened. Then a large bomb destroyed what was left. Nobody ever claimed responsibility but the list of suspects is short.

"Then in an extraordinary decision Israel decided not to allow the Muslims to rebuild and instead said the Temple Mount group should be allowed to build their Jewish temple. The argument went that the Muslims had a temple there for the last 1,400 years and now it was the Jews turn. It has caused a huge rumpus worldwide and a large contingent of soldiers and tanks have had to guard the building site day and night. There have been protests and violence all over the world. I have no idea why the Israelis chose such a provocative action, particularly as the Temple Mount Faithful were one of the prime suspects for the bombing. It is quite inexplicable."

"Oh I know somebody very persuasive who probably had a hand in it," said Alex.

"The last I heard they were only a few months off finishing."

"Then the world ends?"

"Oh no. There are several other prophecies which need to be completed first. The temple will have to be purified first with ash from a flawless red heifer which is going to be tough to find, then the anti-Christ will walk in and declare he is God. Finally a war will start between Israel and her neighbours which will result in the destruction of Damascus. After that the Rapture occurs and the Tribulation begins, cumulating in the end of everything."

"Surely nobody takes people seriously who wander around saying 'The end of the world is nigh'."

"That's where you're wrong. The End Timers are a significant political force in America. They count influential senators among their number and many other politicians include supporters on their staff. In fact many believe that both the President and Vice President are believers, though they were both very careful to duck the issue with stock answers during their election campaigns."

"How come they are not better known?"

"Beats me. They aren't particularly subtle about their intentions. Many End Timers support the building of controversial illegal settlements in the Israeli-occupied territories, encourage conflict with Iran and oppose U.S. sponsored Middle East peace plans."

"That doesn't sound very Christian. What happened to 'Blessed are the Peacemakers'?"

"I would have asked at the meeting but I found myself lying

in a gutter before I got the chance."

"I think I need to go away and think about it. I can't see how all this mumbo-jumbo helps the er... opposition, but meanwhile I've got a friend who has also got some questions for you."

"OK, where are they?"

"Oh, around. The first one is do most religions have one God?"

"Far from it, though the newer ones tend to. However the Hindus have lots and the Buddhists have none."

"Really? I think he would be most interested in a religion without Gods."

The professor walked her through some of the basics but after a while her attention drifted and she had to stifle a yawn. It was a look he was all too familiar with in students so he said, "Maybe we should take a break and continue this another time. You can pop back whenever you want."

"Thanks Prof," she said, then made him regret his words as she popped out of existence in front of his eyes.

15

Dimitri

Just over a month later Dimitri, the Russian Defence Minister, stood up from his desk in the heart of the Kremlin and left the room to get some lunch. He was therefore startled to find himself suddenly back at his desk. Weird. He must have dozed off for a moment and just dreamt of leaving. Deciding to add a strong cup of coffee to his planned meal he stood up to leave once more but the phone on his desk rang before he could take a step.

In truth it was no longer the real Dimitri sitting at his desk but an agent cloned from the man who had left for lunch. Furthermore the phone was not ringing. His ear drums were being vibrated to give that impression, but this copied version of Dimitri was unaware of both these important facts.

SVR is the Russian acronym for the Foreign Intelligence Service who handle espionage and intelligence gathering abroad. When Dimitri picked up his desktop phone it was the head of this organisation whose voice he believed he was hearing.

"It's Lamda, she's broken cover for an emergency message. I have her on the line right now – you need to hear what she has to say first hand."

"Put her on," he ordered. This was most irregular. The identity of a spy is only known to a handful of people and politicians never get to speak to them directly. Lamda was their greatest American asset, a secretary on the President's staff. For her to risk exposure by phoning Russia directly and for the SVR to be prepared to put her through to him could only mean this was extremely serious.

Her voice sounded high pitched and verging on hysteria. "The Americans are about to launch a surprise large scale nuclear strike aimed at Russia and its allies. You must warn the President at once!"

He could scarcely believe his ears. Unaware his ears were indeed betraying him he replied, "Are you absolutely sure? Could you be wrong?"

"No doubt whatsoever. The President's gone mad and the VP is going along with it. You have to do something."

During the two long seconds of fear laden silence that followed he felt a chill travelling down his back and he shivered. There was only one thing he could do. Without another word he slammed the phone down and set off at an unaccustomed sprint in the direction of the President's office. This was not a job for the telephone; the President would need his advice.

Dimitri's clone had not even reached his own office door before he dissolved into a brief swirl of smoke like particles.

16

The Monastry

**Speak unto the children of Israel, that they bring thee a
red heifer without spot, wherein is no blemish, and
upon which never came yoke [Numbers 19:2]**

The monastery where Alex fidgeted was unusual for the region,
being more reminiscent of an ancient Indian Vihara than those
more commonly found here in Laos.

At the base of a horseshoe shaped cliff small rooms had been
carved out of the rock, the silence they afforded making them
well suited for private meditation.

The buildings in front of the cliff were of mixed sizes
and construction, ranging from temporary looking bamboo
structures to sturdy stone. The red robed monks and a golden
statue of Buddha added splashes of colour.

"Something strange just happened in Russia."

"Oh?" said Alex. She was waiting to speak to a monk called
Sommath but he was busy meditating and time was dragging.
Monasteries lack many diversions for an impatient teenage
girl.

"*My brother cloned the Russian Defence Minister, faked a phone call and then destroyed the clone.*"

"Weird. What was the call?"

"*I could not tell what he was hearing, only the Russian's words which were 'Put her on' and 'Are you absolutely sure? Could you be wrong?'*"

"You're not giving me much to go on."

"*That's all there is.*"

"Maybe it was a trick that didn't work out."

"*Maybe.*"

A long silence followed during which Alex untangled knots in the string of a wooden yo-yo Bob had provided for her.

"This is boring."

"*I imagine even 'super heroes' get bored sometimes.*"

"Do you? Get bored I mean."

"*No, I am not capable of it, nor any other emotion.*"

"Have you ever tried thinking in a human brain?"

"*Yes*"

Alex was surprised. "That's possible?"

"*It was a disaster. I tried to process some simple thoughts through the brain of an agent. Synapses tried to fire in opposite directions simultaneously as two minds gave conflicting instructions to one brain. There was a feelings of pain, nausea and a spinning sensation akin to vertigo. It was the only time I have experienced human emotions and it was most unpleasant. My agent was sick for some hours afterwards. I never tried it again.*"

"Has your brother?"

"*I once saw his agent display similar symptoms, so yes I think he tried it too with similar results.*"

"Don't ever try that on me, OK?"

"*I have no intention of doing so.*"

"Good."

She looked around at the monastery for the hundredth time searching for something, anything, to do.

"Is he *still* meditating in there?"

"*Yes*"

Alex sighed, picked up the yo-yo and gave it another go. She did not seem to be getting any better despite all the practice.

"This yo-yo isn't part of me, is it?" she said thoughtfully.

"*No*"

"Doesn't that mean it's draining extra power from you in the same way a second agent would?"

"*No, it is a 'Construct'. In your case I have a channel open providing you with constant power. It allows me to provide you with your 'abilities' and prevents my brother destroying you. Constructs such as that yo-yo require only an insignificant flicker of power to create and have no enduring link. The downside is that my brother could easily destroy it if he wishes.*"

"I assume that applies to the food and drink you give me too. Does that mean I could destroy Ralph's food and make him go hungry?"

"*You could indeed destroy his food and prevent him eating but you can not prevent him receiving nourishment directly into his body. He would almost certainly retaliate and you would both be reduced to a diet of pre-chewed food being inserted directly into your stomachs.*"

"Yuk. I don't fancy that at all."

"*That is an opinion shared by all the agents on both sides to date. A similar truce exists for inconsequential items such as that yo-yo. However let me know if you feel Ralph has been provided with any Construct that gives him an advantage and I will remove it.*"

"Will do."

Alex wound the string back onto the yo-yo, then put it in her lap and sighed deeply again.

"I'm bored. What's Ralph doing?"

"He has completed building the temple and is now struggling with a cow."

"That sounds more fun than this place, let's go and annoy him. We can talk to Sommath later."

"I'm not sure what there is to gain."

"It means I get to annoy him for a while instead of you."

"Very well"

As no monks were looking in her direction Alex promptly vanished into a cloud of molecules which streamed across the planet and reassembled in an outer chamber of the Jewish temple.

"Isn't that cheating?" said Alex to a rather startled Ralph. "I thought it had to be a red heifer, not one you painted red."

"The bible doesn't say it has to be a natural red, as long as the cow is perfect and has never worn a yoke." To tell the truth Ralph was distinctly uncomfortable with the deception and felt much the same way as Alex, but his archangel had reassured him that it would be acceptable.

"What's that? Looks like henna to me. At least the cow's going to smell nice. And that says food colouring, and that over there looks like a genuine pot of paint! Wow. I didn't mean it literally when I said you were painting it red, but you are."

Ralph tried to ignore her.

"What do you do when your friends suggest painting the town red? Do you head out with a bucket and brush?"

"Don't you have any saints to torment, or satanic rituals to perform?" snapped Ralph.

"Nah. They get a bit samey after a while. Have you thought

about getting some of the red colouring on the cow now you've painted the room?"

Ralph gritted his teeth.

17

Nats

Sommath sat motionless in his cell. A long time ago there had been a candle but it had long since burnt out, leaving the small room almost pitch black.

The monk strove to separate himself from the desires and sufferings of everyday life, for they were of no consequence. They sought only to distract him from his search. He thought of Enlightenment as pearls at the bottom of a muddy pool whose surface was being ruffled by the wind. Stilling the water and searching through the mud required concentration and comprehension. The Four Nobles Truths served as a foundation and he lived his life by the principals of the Eight Fold Noble Path. From that starting point he was able to use meditation to calm the ruffled surface of the water, gradually filtering out the distractions. Only once he had combined all these successfully could he reach the mud at the bottom of the pool and begin searching though it for the pearls of wisdom that might eventually allow him to achieve Enlightenment, either in this life or the next.

Around him he was dimly aware of the faint sound of

movement from monks passing in the corridor outside but successfully chose not to process what his ears could hear. There was, however, one wrinkle in his state of single minded stillness. There was somebody in the room with him. He attempted to simply accept it the way he accepted there were four windowless walls around him and one door. The trouble was that the logical side of his brain was refusing to remain dormant, pointing out the only door into the room made a fearful creaking sound, but he had heard nothing. Gradually, however, he managed to regain control and bring the puzzle into acceptance. The question and its answer were of no consequence.

"Are you going to be much longer 'cos this place gives me the creeps?"

A young girl's voice. A teenager perhaps. She stepped in front of him where a thin crack of light from the uneven door frame allowed just enough illumination for another puzzle. The girl was Caucasian yet spoke fluent Lao. Most unusual.

The world was intruding so in a change of strategy he abandoned his attempt to find a deeper meditative state. Instead would try to retain what he had achieved and take it out into the world even as he spoke, bathed and ate. He felt no annoyance at the disturbance, this simply was what was, and he accepted it as such.

"Perhaps it is time for me to be tested", he said at last.

"Does that mean it's OK to ask you some questions?"

"Yes"

"Everybody says you are the best guy around at meditating, so I wanted to ask you why and how you do it."

"No one can judge something as internal as meditation and say one person is better than another."

"Well everybody round here says you are dead good at it and can do it for days at a time. Plus they say you are good at teaching novices what to do."

"I am grateful for the respect of my peers, undeserved though it is. As to how you do it, your goal is pure single mindedness of thought. There are over fifty methods for developing mindfulness and forty for developing concentration. Whichever route you choose at some point you will need to clear your mind and think about nothing at all, which is challenging."

"Doesn't sound so hard."

"Try now. Empty your mind and do not allow a single thought to enter."

She tried briefly but in just a few seconds a barrage of thoughts had swirled around her head. "Hmm. It's harder than you'd think."

"Oh I know how hard it is."

"Yeah but I've got more on my mind. You don't have to save the world."

"I try, one soul at a time. I teach novices. May I ask you a question?"

"Me? Sure."

"Are you a Nat?"

Alex felt a swirling confusion at the name. Clearly the word was an important one to the person whose language centre Bob had copied, but she lacked the memories it was trying to activate. The effect was disconcerting.

"A what?" she managed to say, putting a hand out to steady herself against the wall.

It occurred to Sommath that if she did not know what the word meant it was unlikely she was one, but he had also not missed the effect the word had on her.

"Nats are spirits of the earth. They inhabit trees, rocks and other natural homes. When their homes are removed to make way for a building, such as this monastery, they are displaced and unhappy. Chaotic and impulsive they can cause trouble so people appease them by building a replacement spirit house outside the building and making offerings at it every morning. The belief in Nats has become incorporated into Buddhism throughout the region.

"I came to the conclusion that the belief is erroneous and a distraction from our studies. I managed to persuade the Head Monk to remove the monastery's spirit house but now I am beginning to think it was a mistake."

"Oh no, not me. I'm no Nat, I'm just an… um…" It occurred to her she was not 'just an ordinary girl' as she had been about to say. "I'm Alex," she said simply, then realised even that was not strictly true.

The monk did not look convinced by her answer.

"Listen, before I forget I've got a question about Buddhism. If you don't have gods or anything then what is nirvana and who…?"

"We should go. The temple is about to be consecrated."

"Consecrated? What's that?"

"Officially opened."

"Damn. You mean I've got a splitting headache from learning Lao and now it's back to Hebrew again?" Then she turned to the confused monk and said, as if by way of explanation, "It's the tonal languages - I can't seem to get my head round them."

The monk did his best to let the senseless words drift pass him unquestioned and said nothing.

"OK, let's go," she said with resignation. Then to the monk,

"Got to run, see you later, Sommath."

She stepped back out of his line of vision and was gone. The door made no creaking sound. Acceptance was going to be a real struggle, he could tell. Maybe he should go and see if the novices had left him anything to eat.

18

Temple Mount

**For there shall arise false Christs, and false prophets,
and shall shew great signs and wonders; insomuch that,
if it were possible, they shall deceive the very elect.
[Matthew 24:24]**

On the shallow summit of Temple Mount stood the newly completed Third Jewish Temple, built over the ruins of the Islamic 'Dome of the Rock' mosque. Around it miles of barbed wire fences and troops kept large crowds of protesters well away.

Inside the temple Ralph looked dejectedly at Alex sitting in one of the pews beside the aisle. She waved at him cheerily but he was not inclined to wave back.

Yesterday she had made a complete mockery of the slaughter of the red heifer, piping up regularly and loudly with unhelpful comments such as, "Oh that cow smells divine. I love the smell of henna, don't you?" and, "Wow. That is one red heifer. Even its footprints are red."

Two uniformed security guards built like tanks had grabbed

her and tried to drag her out. She might have well been made of stone and bolted to the floor as to their surprise they were unable to move her, even though she was not apparently holding on to anything. Ralph had waved them off before she became the centre of attention even more than she already was. She had giggled and called after their retreating backs, "Don't feel bad. I think I just ate too many chocolate chip cookies."

Now here she was again, and today was much more important. The ashes from the cremated cow were ready to consecrate the priests, the temple and the more important religious items. Worse, unlike yesterday the world's media had turned up including TV crews from CNN, BBC and Al Jazeera. If she made his moment of triumph into a farce he would... well actually he couldn't think of anything he could do, but he would do it just as soon as he came up with something.

However to Ralph's surprise she largely behaved herself. True, she did try to 'accidentally' sneeze on the ashes as they were being processed past her but the priest had been nimble enough to protect them with his body and prevent any being lost.

It was a magnificent occasion. 120 lay priests wore garments woven by master craftsmen. Their robes, waist sashes and turbans were all a light yellow. The High Priest also wore robes but they were sky blue and white, worn beneath a backwards facing multi-coloured apron known as an ephod and a square breastplate. Over the turban he wore the Tzitz, a dazzling crown of pure gold with the words 'Holy to the Lord' engraved across it. Small bells sown into the hem of his robe jangled softly as he walked.

Ralph felt the outfits were perfect. They were far from the gaudy, spectacular look a Western designer might have chosen. The clothing was relatively simple, dignified and exquisitely crafted, perfectly satisfying the biblical requirement that they be 'for glory and for beauty'.

The ritual had started an hour earlier with the ashes of the heifer being used to purify the priests before their entry into the temple. Now, with all the steps complete, the High Priest was ready to bring the ceremony to a close with his final announcement.

"I declare this temple consecrated and ready for the worship of God," he concluded triumphantly.

The congregation and media thought it was all over. There were sounds of people shifting as they got ready to process out after the priests and the TV crews prepared to switch back to their studios, but to everybody's surprise it turned out to be just the beginning.

Suddenly a bearded, wild eyed man appeared out of thin air on top of the altar. Even he looked slightly startled for a moment before recovering and declaring to the stunned congregation and TV crews, "I am God, worship me in earnest for the end of the world is come."

19

Anti-Christ

When ye therefore shall see the abomination of desolation, spoken of by Daniel the prophet, stand in the holy place... then shall be great tribulation, such as was not since the beginning of the world to this time, no, nor ever shall be.
[Matthew 24:15-21]

"He is an opposition agent," said Bob.

"I guessed," growled back Alex, "but Ralph is still here. I thought he only ever used one agent at most."

"Until now. You may now summon a second if you wish."

Alex thought about fetching the Old Man but was not sure how to use him.

"Maybe in a moment. Right now tell me who he is." Bob did as she asked and then Alex stood up and yelled out loudly.

"His name is Albert Marshall, he is currently undergoing treatment at Ontario Shores in Canada for a God complex."

The congregation could hear her well enough as could the reporters, but the TV cameras were equipped with directional microphones to avoid background noise and they were aimed at the figure on the altar. The TV audience could hear faint, indistinct shouting in the background, but that hardly surprised them considering a figure claiming to be God had just popped into existence.

The trouble with 24 hour news reporting on TV is that breaking news goes out unchecked. The TV crews were accompanied by reporters who were professionals and were duly noting down what Alex was saying. Later they would make some calls and, if it checked out, use it in a follow up piece. That, however, was later and all that mattered was what was happening right now.

Albert was in his element. Not only did he have the undivided attention of a huge worldwide audience but he could hear the voice of the Holy Spirit talking to him in his head. It guided his words and even provided biblical quotations to support them, though he did have a tendency to embellish the message he was meant to be giving. Now at last the doubters would realise he truly was God, as he had always insisted. He was ecstatic.

"I thought you said Lucifer was always careful not to reveal the presence of you both," said Alex.

"That has been the case for thousands of years. He has not revealed us because he fears mankind, and I have not done so to avoid influencing the people I wished to study."

"So what's changed?"

"I believe we are seeing the endgame. Whatever the plan may be it is almost complete and he is confident of winning."

Alex desperately tried to think. Everything was suddenly happening too fast. She was all too aware she was close to losing without having even discovered what the game was. Then she remembered what Professor Dalton had said. After the temple was built Satan would appear and pretend to be God. The audience were not meant to believe what Albert was saying, they were meant to think he was lying.

"It's the anti-Christ," she breathed, "but surely your brother doesn't believe that by simply fulfilling all the prophecies the world will end?"

"No, he does not. However note that the only unfulfilled prophecy left is the war."

Alex looked across at Ralph. She was just in time to hear him say, "OK, I'm ready", before he vanished into thin air.

"Wherever he's gone take me there as quickly as you can," she ordered.

20

Oval Office

For the Lord himself shall descend from heaven with a shout, with the voice of the archangel, and with the trump of God
[I Thessalonians 4:16-17]

It was just after 4 a.m. in Washington but despite the unsociable hour both the President and Vice President were wide awake in the Oval Office and glued to the live CNN feed from the temple.

The men were very different. The President was a short and intense man, always determined to get his way. His school nickname, Napoleon, still plagued him but it was a long time since any one had dared say it to his face. George, his Vice President, was taller and more rotund with a genial and deferential manner.

As a team they had proved unstoppable. George went on ahead and did his best to open doors in their path before his friend arrived to kick them down, and smoothed any feathers ruffled in their passing. He was content to play second fiddle and in doing so had followed his friend to the very top.

"This is it, George," said the President in an uneven voice. "The Second Coming."

His fists were bunched next to his chest which felt ready to burst with excitement.

"Absolutely, Mr President," replied George. Although they were life long friends the man steadfastly refused to call him anything other than 'Mr President' ever since he had taken office, even in private. George sounded no less eager because, as Professor Dalton had suspected, they were both committed End Timers.

"The only event left is the war which will include the destruction of Damascus. I don't think it can be far away. I wonder what will trigger it."

"You will," said a voice behind him and they spun around to find themselves face to face with an angel. Wings sprouted from his back, a halo shone above his head and his whole body radiated with light.

"You are the chosen instrument of God, you will wield the sword, you will fulfil God's ancient promise to his chosen people and bring about the Second Coming."

Both men fell to their knees before the heavenly figure. As they did so there was a sudden whip like crack and a wave of warm air swept over them as a second figure snapped into existence.

Normally Bob moved Alex in and out of populated areas at sub-sonic speeds to avoid being noticed. However she had made the unfortunate demand that he move her as quickly as possible, so her entry into the room was accompanied by the crack of a miniature sonic boom. On top of that the air displaced by her accelerated reassembly into human form caused a pressure wave strong enough to rattle the windows.

All in all it was the worst way imaginable to appear to religious men kneeling before an angel. A fact Ralph could not resist pointing out.

"Ah, right on cue the agent of Satan arrives with a thunderbolt. Until the Second Coming and the final reckoning such things remain in balance and its presence is inevitable. I urge you to ignore anything it says. It has been sent by the Father of Lies."

The men, still on their knees, turned their attention away and bowed their heads again before the angel.

"I'm a 'she', not an 'it', and you can stop grovelling," said Alex, "that's only Ralph with a light job." Then to the middle distance she added, "Can we do anything about that?"

"The light is internal, I can not prevent it. The wings are non-functional but are extruded from the body so I can not remove them either, however the halo is an external construct."

"Then lose it," she commanded, and Ralph's halo winked out of existence. The men had their heads bowed so they missed both its disappearance and the look of irritation Ralph shot Alex.

Ralph recovered well and continued as if nothing had happened, speaking with authority, "Know that I am the voice of an archangel and have been dispatched to tell you the Lord is on his way, as predicted in the Bible."

"The first book of Thessalonians, Chapter 4 verse 16," said the President. It was one he knew by heart. "For the Lord himself shall descend from heaven with a shout, with the voice of the archangel, and with the trump of God."

In the moment's silence that followed Albert's voice could be heard from the TV across the room. He was basking in the attention, though his flowery language had become all but incomprehensible.

"What would you have us do?" the President asked Ralph.

"You must smite all the foreigners occupying the Promised Land. Use enough nuclear weapons to make sure none survive for God long since promised it to his people and the promise must be fulfilled before the end."

The President was startled. "But millions will die and the radiation will make the land useless to Israel."

"Your thinking is woefully blinkered. Promises from God are always fulfilled. The cost is irrelevant for I tell you now not a single righteous person shall suffer. They shall all be Raptured. The rest will either die or live to suffer the seven years of Tribulation that will follow before the final end. So it is written. So it will be."

Ralph was utterly convincing because he believed every word of it. He spoke with complete assurance and his words were compelling.

"I apologise, I would not dream of questioning God's will, I was just surprised for a second," said the President in an uncharacteristically humble voice. "I am also ashamed to admit I do not know the exact boundaries of the Promised Land."

"From the river of Egypt as far as the great river, the river Euphrates, Genesis chapter 15 verse 18," said Ralph, adding helpfully, "I have a map". He handed over a piece of parchment. It showed not only the boundaries of the Promised Land, but the latitude and longitude of every target requiring a missile. He was clearly well prepared.

"My God," exclaimed the Vice President after studying it, then hastily and profusely apologised to the angel for his blasphemy. "It's just that this list includes some of Egypt, some of Syria, all of Jordan, plus some of Saudi Arabia and Iraq. Some of these are allies of the U.S."

"The righteous will be saved," repeated Ralph.

The President paused, as he always did before making any momentous decision, though in this case the path was laid out so clearly in truth there was nothing to decide. "As God wills, so it shall be."

"What!" exclaimed Alex. "You mean you actually swallowed all this horseshit?"

The men ignored her. She was at a loss, realising she was talking to three religious fanatics whose thinking she could not comprehend. She could argue logic and ethics all day without making the slightest impression. Alex had not the faintest idea what to do next.

The President pressed the intercom button and said, "Send in the Football."

21

The Football

Major Mitchell was a career soldier. It was all he had ever wanted to do. He was an effective soldier and a man of integrity, honour and duty, but had started to believe those qualities were becoming a hindrance. As he rose higher up the chain of command he found his soldiering skills becoming less important. Political skill was needed instead. He could not order people to do things that obviously needed doing. Instead they had to be gently persuaded and even then watered down compromises unsatisfactory to everyone were the almost inevitable outcome. This was not in his nature or skill set so he had resigned himself to the belief he could progress no further when he was unexpectedly handed the best assignment in the world - the 'Carrier'.

As Carrier he got to fly all round the world meeting the rich and powerful, visiting countries he sometimes had to consult an atlas to find. He stayed in hotels he could never dream of affording, sleeping in the room right next door to the President and saw spectacular welcoming ceremonies from the same viewpoints as the heads of state. He would retire when this assignment ended because nothing could ever top it.

Handcuffed to his wrist was a chain leading to a briefcase. It was known as the 'Football' and contained everything the President needed to launch the nuclear arsenal. As Carrier it was up to him to make sure he was never more than a room away from the President.

When the President's summons arrived he was awake and alert despite the early hour. Doubtless the President would be moving. There had been embarrassing moments with previous Presidents when they had jumped into cars leaving the Carrier behind, and in doing so left America unable to respond to a nuclear attack for unacceptably long periods of time. Fortunately it had not happened to him. At least not yet.

Mitchell stepped inside the Oval Office, the briefcase chained as always to his wrist. Having been stationed outside he knew who ought to be in the room, so he stopped short when he saw a girl and an alarmingly glowing man with wings. Without pausing he whirled round to the doorway where two Secret Service agents were on guard outside, dressed in identical dark suits with poorly hidden earpieces. He only had to say a single word to bring them running in. "Intruders."

A civilian would take time to change from a state of relaxed boredom to full alertness, but these men took none. They were running in and drawing weapons almost before Mitchell had finished speaking. Neither were they fazed by the unexpected sight of a girl and an angel.

"Get down on the floor and put your hands behind your heads. Do it NOW!" one shouted.

Alex and Ralph did not even bother looking round. As both targets were empty handed they charged instead of shooting, intending to wrestle them to the floor and cuff them. What actually happened was they struck bodies that felt as if they were made of granite and bounced off painfully.

"Enough," said the President. The demonstration had removed his last shred of doubt. "These are clearly supernatural beings of good and evil, I doubt very much there is anything you can do to harm them."

"No," said Ralph

"No," said Alex, in rare agreement, "but don't look at me when you say 'evil'. Just because he washes his clothes with Persil doesn't make him an angel."

The agents looked on dubiously. The senior man stopped rubbing his shoulder and raised his wrist microphone to his mouth but the President quickly said, "Please don't call for any more security, it won't make any difference and a room full of agitated Secret Service agents will only get in the way."

The agent hesitated. They did not have to obey the President when it came to an issue of personal security but as the intruders appeared unarmed and non-aggressive he saw no immediate threat. Reluctantly he assented, but insisted they both remain in the room. He also fully intended to call for reinforcements the moment he felt there was a need, regardless of the President's wishes.

The President called Major Mitchell over, handed him the map and issued the orders. Alex thought the Major's eyes would pop out of his head.

"B-but why?" stammered Mitchell. "As far as I know there

has been no threat made against the U.S."

"Because I have it on the highest authority, the *very* highest authority, that it is necessary."

"Please don't tell me it's because an 'angel' told you to do it. Surely you don't want to start a nuclear war because of a conjuring trick?"

Alex felt like cheering but in a rare moment of restraint decided it might not help the Major's cause to be seen to ally with him.

The President was growing angry. "You will do it because I told you to. That is all the authority you need. It is not your decision, it is mine. Do not question me again. Open the Football."

The President was right. The Major had absolutely no authority over the decision; he was there purely to carry out the President's wishes. There was just one card left to play; he needed to get more people involved who were authorised to advise the President and make him see sense.

"Very well, sir. However there is no need to use the Football here in the White House, if we relocate to the Situation Room you can fire from there and receive up to date worldwide information."

The President spotted the trap. He already knew what needed to be done and the last thing he wanted was to spend hours arguing about it with generals and other unbelievers.

"No, I want to see this out from the Oval Office. I already know all I need to know and you can handle the communications from here."

Mitchell had taken it to the line. Duty would allow him to delay no further. Reluctantly he unlocked and opened the case. There were a set of nuclear options which it was now his job to explain to the President, ranging from a single cruise missile to a full strike.

He began but the President cut him off saying, "There is no need to explain these. You have already been given the plan including the number of missiles to fire and their coordinates."

"Very well, sir. However may I point out the number of missiles is excessive. You are planning to fire two thirds of our arsenal at an area short of targets, much of it desert. We could do it with much less."

"We stick to the plan," he insisted.

"Very well, sir. We currently have very few missiles targeted on the region so we will need to reprogram them."

"How long will that take?"

"Well… we will need to divide the targets between ICBMs and SLBMs. Fortunately the Phase II upgrades have just been applied to both the REACT and SRS systems…"

The President sighed. Military men always started talking in alphabets when they were under stress but he had long since found the perfect antidote, he simply repeated the original question at half the speed with twice the emphasis. It worked wonders.

"How. Long. Will. That. Take."

"Sorry, Sir," said Mitchell, realising in his contemplation he had not actually supplied a figure. "I think we can reprogram enough missiles in the next 25 minutes to execute your plan."

Not my plan, thought the President, God's plan. But he held his tongue, Mitchell would not have understood.

"Do it."

Mitchell summoned a runner and handed over the target list to take to the Situation Room. Then he used the SATCOM phone in the briefcase to advise them the list was on the way and to verify its authenticity. The secure phone served to confirm his identity as only the Situation Room had the codes required to unscramble the encrypted signal it generated. Even so there was an argument, as he had known there would be, and it took the President to take over the call and make it clear in no uncertain terms what his wishes were before they finally conceded.

"A thought," said the Vice President. "When we launch the Russians might think we are shooting at them and return fire. Not that it matters if the world is ending soon, but I would feel uncomfortable about leaving such a legacy after our Rapture. Many people would still have another seven years to live, and believers or not they are still American citizens."

"Very unlikely," said the Major. This was the one silver lining he had been able to think of in the whole mess. "Rehearsals and studies by the Russians have revealed that in practice they have only three to four minutes to make a decision after detecting a launch before it is too late. In addition the Early Warning Systems of both sides are notoriously unreliable and easily confused by satellites, meteors, solar flares and a host of other innocent causes. Heck, throughout the 80's our EWS triggered alerts an average of six times a day. Considering the current good relations between our two countries I believe the Russians will hesitate to believe their instruments. They have only to pause for a moment, which they will do by phoning you on the Hot Line, before it will become clear the missiles are not headed for them and the moment of danger will pass. I suggest not calling them in advance as if they do not believe you it would give them an opportunity to fire that they would otherwise lack."

"Very well," said the President, relieved that he would not

go down in what remained of history as the President that destroyed America.

"Madness," muttered Alex, then to Bob, "Will this end the world?"

"Not if the Russians do not fire. The loss of life will be great but even the excessive number of missiles in their plan will be insufficient to trigger a lasting nuclear winter. As long as it remains contained the human race will survive."

But at that very moment, five thousand of miles away, the Dimitri clone snapped back into existence in the same position he had been occupying four days previously and, unaware of the lost days, carried on sprinting breathlessly towards the heart of the Kremlin.

22

Reaction

Compared to the Oval Office the Working Residence of the Russian President in the Kremlin is less grand but benefits from a workmanlike air. The room is simply lined with oak panelling and plenty of bookshelves, though the eye is drawn to the impressive twin chandeliers. The President's desk lies near the far end, flanked by the flags of the Russian Federation and the Presidential standard. The views are wonderful, a panoramic view of the Moskva River to the south, famous Red Square to the east and the charming Alexander Gardens to the west.

For larger meetings there is a table with seating for seven. However there were only two people in the room at noon when Dimitri burst in unannounced, the President behind his working desk and his Personal Assistant seated opposite, slowly working through the afternoon agenda.

The real Dimitri was downstairs in Conference Room 1 discussing the details of an upcoming military exercise, but nobody was aware of the fact, least of all Dimitri's clone.

"Apologies, Mr President," he burst out somewhat breathlessly, "but our top agent just broke cover to tell us the American President has authorised a surprise nuclear strike against our country. They will open fire in a matter of minutes."

"What!? Why on earth would they do that? What is there to gain? Our relations with them recently have been about as good as they get."

"I can only think that is the very reason. We've long known an unexpected first strike by either country would cripple the other's ability to respond unless they acted very fast indeed. Something unlikely to occur when relations are good and defences relaxed. We would think it much more likely our instruments were at fault than a completely unprovoked attack was under way."

Both men knew the limitations of their instruments as there had been many false alarms. In 1983 at a time of high tensions the Russians detected 5 incoming nukes and conducted 30 extra checks to confirm the launch was genuine, all of which confirmed it was. Fortunately the man in charge had so little faith in the system he disobeyed orders and did not pass on the alert. It turned out to be sunlight reflecting off clouds. Then in 1995 a rocket test on a Norwegian Island was mistaken for a submarine launched missile. This time President Yeltsin was informed and he got as far as opening the 'black case' required to launch a Russian retaliation before they finally realised the almost catastrophic error. They knew the Americans had suffered similar such dangerous embarrassments too.

The President was an intelligent and passionate man. Intelligent enough to see the inescapable logic and passionate enough to be almost speechless with indignation and betrayal.

"They couldn't... they wouldn't..." but he knew they could, and if the man in charge was cynical enough perhaps they would. He had felt uneasy about the American President ever since meeting him. He had seen a burning fanaticism in the man's eyes that reminded him of the Chechen rebels he had fought in the army, many years before.

He took a deep breath, paused and thought for a moment.

"Wait. What if this turns out to be a double agent? Perhaps some third party is trying to set us at each others throats. They may well have another agent telling the Americans it is us who are about to fire. If the Americans see us go to maximum alert it could trigger the very conflict we fear."

It was a good point and one that Dimitri realised he should have considered, but he recovered quickly.

"There is a protocol for situations like this," he said.

"Of course there is," said the President with a short, humourless, bark like laugh. All the military seemed to do all day was sit around planning responses to ever more unlikely scenarios. "Tell me."

"I'll have the details fetched but essentially we go to the highest state of alert possible without tipping off the Americans. Submarines submerge at a depth suitable for both firing and radio reception. Nuclear bombs are loaded onto planes and crews man them, but they remain on the ground in hangers. ICBMs are fuelled and primed ready for launch but the missile bay doors remain closed. Key holders are contacted and remain in contact with cases open and the Main Operational Directorate calls all missile centres to be sure they are standing by ready to receive instructions. All the actions are non-provocative but will allow us to respond swiftly if it turns out to be true."

The President mulled it over. It made perfect sense. It was non-aggressive but would prevent them being caught unawares by any treacherous American attack. Furthermore if they were indeed being played, and he had a nagging feeling they were, this would thwart whatever evil plans had been hatched.

"Do it."

23

Too Fast

"Alex, a third opposition agent has appeared in the Kremlin and told the Russian President that America is about to attack them."

"What? Until a moment ago he never had more than one agent at a time, and now he's got three running around?"

"Yes. You may also summon two more."

"I would if I knew what to do with them. This is all happening too fast."

"An update. The Russians have prepared a nuclear response but will not shoot first."

Alex did her best to tell the American President that the Russians were gearing up for war but he was not very interested in anything she had to say and Ralph kept interrupting to say all her words were lies.

Frustrated she whispered to Bob, "Use that hologram thing you said the Old Man developed and show them the Russian President being informed." Then out loud she said, "Watch this."

Her body vanished to be replaced with an Alex shaped hole in the air. A window through which the scene in Russia could be viewed. It was even possible to walk round and see the perspective change.

They watched Dimitri running breathlessly down a corridor and into a reception area. Startled guards gripped their rifles then recognised him and relaxed. A secretary tried to intercept him but he ran past and burst into the Russian President's office saying, "Apologies, Mr President, but our top agent just broke cover to tell us the American President has authorised a surprise nuclear attack against our country. They will open fire in a matter of minutes."

They all saw the look of shock on the Russian President's face before the image vanished and Alex snapped back into view.

Meanwhile Ralph had been doing some whispering of his own and before anyone could react he said smartly, "The demon can show you any image it chooses. Just because the images look lifelike doesn't mean they are real. Watch."

Then he too was gone and in the hole where he had stood they could see themselves standing in the Oval Office. The only difference was that in this picture Alex was clutching a glass of orange juice with a straw. She put it to her mouth and sucked, only to have the contents squirt comically out of her ears. The point made Ralph snapped back into sight.

"That's amazing," said George.

"It certainly is," said Alex. "Who would ever have suspected that Ralph had a sense of humour?"

Clearly Alex's 'proof' was no such thing, but even so the President found himself unsettled by Dimitri's desperate words.

Holding up his hand for silence he said, "Major, how much longer until the reprogramming is complete?"

"Fourteen minutes."

"Then that is how long you have to tell me what the Russians are up to."

"At once, sir."

The Major grabbed the President's desk phone and started making urgent calls. The President kept eyeing the Hot Line and wondering if he should be using it. After just eleven minutes Major had all the answers he needed.

He turned to the President and reported, "Their bombers are on the ground, plus satellites looking at an admittedly small sample of ICBM sites show the hatch covers closed. The only unusual behaviour we have seen is naval. Two ballistic missile submarines in dock scrambled to launch, one diving before it had even fully cleared the harbour. However given the lack of any other indications or movement of troops our opinion is that it was just a local drill."

The President was reassured. The original plan not to tip off the Russians with the Hot Line was the right one.

Ralph wore a 'told you so' expression. Alex looked tired and lost.

24

The Watcher

**If therefore thou shalt not watch, I will come on thee as
a thief, and thou shalt not know what hour I will come
upon thee.**
[Revelation 3:3]

He had been born Sergei, but had lived in America for so long
the name felt unfamiliar. It belonged to another life, somebody
else's life.

Some people claim they have dedicated their whole lives
to their country, when all they really mean is their working
hours. Sergei really had dedicated his life to the cause. He
had abandoned everything familiar and gone to live with the
enemy. If he had stayed in Russia he could have spent his
evenings drinking vodka with friends and holidaying at the
Black Sea resorts. Instead he lived a life of isolation thousands
of miles away from the country he loved. He had been forced to
watch nervously from afar as Russia changed drastically under
Gorbachev, teetered under Yeltsin, and grew strong again under
Putin and the present incumbent.

True, living in America had its compensations; his standard of living was better than it had been at home but no amount of money would ever weaken his loyalty to his country or deflect him from his mission. A mission he earnestly hoped there would never be a need for.

For a moment the early morning phone call that woke him was a simple annoyance, but the moment he heard his secret name he was wide awake and his old life came flooding back. A code word was given and passed back and the call ended abruptly. There was no need to give instructions, Sergei knew exactly what to do. It was the mission he had always dreaded.

He went out and walked round to the back of the isolated gas station he owned and unlocked an old, rusting shed. Inside amongst the rubbish was a large, ordinary looking metal case, also rather rusted. However inside that was a block of concrete into which was embedded a small, smart safe completely out of keeping with its surroundings. He dialled the combination and carefully removed the contents. He inserted a clip into a revolver, checked the safely catch and tucked it into his waist band. Two spare clips went into his pocket. The other items were a pair of military specification image intensifying binoculars and an encrypted satellite phone.

He took them all and walked back outside into the cool, arid Montana night. Leaning up against the main gas station building was a wooden ladder which he used to climb onto the corrugated iron roof.

In front of the ageing pumps lay the road and beyond that a tall fence topped with barbed wire marking the edge of Malmstrom Air Force Base. He settled down, took out the heavy binoculars and took a long look. Then he began carefully and slowly sweeping them from side to side.

25

Point of No Return

**And I will shew wonders in the heavens and in the earth,
blood, and fire, and pillars of smoke.**
[Joel 2:30]

When he had first worn the 'Biscuit' the U.S. President had been constantly aware of it pressing against his skin. Gradually, though, familiarity made him less and less aware until he no longer gave it a second thought. Until now that was. As the time remaining turned from minutes to seconds he could think of little else.

The Biscuit is a small piece of laminated plastic on which the "Gold Codes" are printed. In conjunction with the Football it is all that is needed to release the safety locks on the nuclear arsenal. It is never to leave his person and nobody else is permitted to see it, least of all the Carrier. There had been embarrassments in the past. President Carter used to keep it in his suit pocket until one day he forgot to take it out before the suit went to the dry cleaners. For an uncomfortably long period of time America would have struggled to respond to an attack. After hearing that story the current President had come up with the simple solution of hanging it around his neck.

"We are ready, Mr President," said Major Mitchell.

"Don't do this," pleaded Alex, and the Major joined in adding his voice to hers, but the President silenced them with an upheld hand.

"I'm ready to launch," he stated, "God's will be done."

With that he took off his tie and undid the top two buttons of his shirt revealing the cord around his neck. He tugged on it, pulling the Biscuit high enough to grab. Then he snapped open the opaque cover and pulled out a piece of plastic the size of a credit card on which were a column of ten numbers. Some of them were fakes and would invalidate the authorisation if read out, but the President knew well which ones to avoid.

The Major handed him the handset for the SATCOM and the President began to read out the numbers from the Biscuit in a surprisingly steady voice.

Alex shouted out, "3, 9, 34.9, 33 and a third," trying to distract him or force a mistake, but the President remained completely calm and focused. It was a ten digit number which the officer at the other end typed into his console under careful supervision. A green light lit in front of him.

"Code accepted. Please put the Carrier on the phone for confirmation."

The President was surprised. This had never been part of any past drills. It was news to almost everybody including the officer he was speaking to who had just opened sealed orders. There was a good reason for the extreme secrecy as the extra step existed because the military doubted the courage of the President. Not this President in particular but all Presidents. The military felt that men who gain office do so for reasons of political skill or public appeal, not valour. In a way it takes courage to stand for office, but not the sort of courage that means anything to a military man.

The weakness of the Football system is that it depends on just one man, and the nightmare scenario for the military would be a President held at gunpoint and ordered to launch or die. In the end they simply did not trust a politician enough to make the right decision in such circumstances, so when the President orders a first strike using the remote Football there are secret orders requiring an additional step.

The phone was handed over to the Carrier. Now all Major Mitchell had to do was say one simple sentence and the missiles would be ready to fire. This was so wrong he felt he had to make one last attempt to bring some sanity back into the room. He did not seriously expect it to work and it would certainly cost him his job but that was of little consequence now. Turning to the Vice President he said, "Sir, if you were to declare the President's mental state impaired under the 25th Amendment I would be prepared to accept your orders over his."

Alex crossed her fingers, the President went red but was so angry he was struck momentarily speechless with indignation. The Vice President stepped smoothly into the breach and replied, "The President is in the best of health both physically and mentally. Furthermore even if I were in charge I would give the same orders."

"Major Mitchell!" thundered the President, still unable to know where to begin berating the officer.

Mitchell took no notice. He was a man of integrity and knew this was wrong, but firmly believed duty took precedence over his own personal opinions. Although he had never realised it that was precisely why he had been chosen for the role.

"My personal identification code is CATZ, spelt C-A-T-Z. I confirm the President is not acting under duress," he said into the handset.

"Acknowledged. Ready to fire," came the response.

At this moment the release codes were sweeping out into the silos and submarines. Individual commanders could now launch simply by turning dual keys, though of course they would wait for the order.

He handed the phone back to the President. "All you have to do now is tell them to execute the plan we set up for you. Its name is 'Middle East Scenario G1.'"

This was it; this was the end of the road. Time for desperate measures. Alex launched herself across the room in a grab for the phone and pandemonium ensued.

Ralph leaped forward and grabbed her wrist. Alarmed by the sudden movement of Alex and Ralph towards the President both the Secret Service agents in the room whipped up their weapons. Feet apart with both hands gripping the guns they started firing. Both were excellent shots and at point blank range none of the shots were going anywhere but into their targets. Alex could feel her skin harden in discs as Bob anticipated the trajectory of each bullet. She hardly felt the impact as they struck, crumpled and fell. Suspecting both adversaries were wearing body armour the agents switched to head shots. It made no difference except now the hardening of the skin on both Alex and Ralph was visible as a brief flicker of grey as each shot was countered.

Alex continued to strain forward to reach the phone that was held just inches away by the President, too shocked to react, but Ralph's hand pulled back with equal force on her wrist leaving them in stalemate.

The agents kept firing until their guns were empty. In the sudden silence that followed as they struggled to reload Alex gave up and let her arm be pulled back with a cry of frustration. The President recovered from his shock and took a step back lifting the phone to his mouth.

"Execute Middle East Scenario G1. Launch now."

26

The Beginning of the End

The burden of Damascus. Behold, Damascus is taken away from being a city, and it shall be a ruinous heap.
[Isaiah 17:1]

At Malmstrom Air Force base a hatch slid open and smoke erupted from it. From within the swirling mass the silhouette of a large missile climbed upwards and then the night was lit up by a huge spurt of flame as it cleared the silo and powered upwards. The first stage booster rocket fired for 60 seconds accelerating its huge bulk at an ever increasing speed. Once expended it dropped away and the second stage motor ignited, continuing the acceleration of the shorter, lighter missile. All around it more missiles were flying upwards in unison until all 500 were airborne. Soon the submarine based Trident missiles would follow.

* * *

From the roof of his remote gas station Sergei saw three stars trailing smoke lift up into the night sky. Beyond them he could see more lights on the horizon, but less distinctly. He guessed other agents would be stationed around the base, and also at Minot and F.G Warren Air Force bases where the rest of the ICBMs were, not that it made any difference to him or his job.

Sergei picked up the phone and pressed a Quick Dial button, he was through in seconds.

He gave a code word followed by "Three plus missiles sighted. It is night time but visibility is excellent. No doubt at all."

He received a curt acknowledgement and the phone went dead. He shivered suddenly in the cold night air.

* * *

Two minutes had passed since the first ICBM launched from its silo. The second stage expired and explosive bolts detached it. A moment later the third stage ignited and the missile climbed ever higher and faster out of the thinning atmosphere, rushing eagerly towards Damascus.

27

Response

But the end of all things is at hand...
[1 Peter 4:7]

In Russia Dimitri yelled down the phone. "You don't make political judgements, that's not your job. In future just tell us the facts." As he slammed the phone down it occurred to him there was unlikely to be a next time.

"Sir, the Early Warning System reports heat signatures throughout the American ICBM network. They rate it as a 'Probable Large Scale Launch', though the idiots tried to downgrade it to 'Possible' solely due to the current lack of tension."

The Russian President felt icy fingers travelling down his spine. "I wouldn't trust their computers to speak my weight. I need confirmation."

"We will have it very soon, sir."

The phone rang again and he relayed the message it brought to the President. "So far six of our nine agents on the ground have reported in and confirmed missile launches. At the least this is a large scale strike, it may even be a full launch. There is no longer any doubt."

"The treachery is breathtaking," breathed the President.

For years he had believed and assured others that nuclear weapons would keep the peace, and they would only ever be used as a desperate last resort. Now both those beliefs had turned out to be untrue.

He glanced at the red Hot Line phone on his desk. What was the point? What was there left to say?

He and Dimitri already had their Black Cases open in front of them. Dimitri's case had taken some finding as for some inexplicable reason the aide who was meant to always follow him around had been sitting outside Conference Room 1. The fool thought Dimitri was in a meeting there.

Without another word he typed in his memorised five digit code and pressed 'Send'. That caused the case in front of Dimitri light up and sound a buzzer. His Defence Minister quickly typed his own five digit code and also pressed the Send button.

The Chief of the General Staff was not present in the office but had been fully briefed so when the combined 10 digit code arrived at his terminal he was ready for it and swifty added his personal code to the end. As he pressed the final Send button the combined 15 digit number was transmitted to the Main Operational Directorate, or the G.O.U. to use its Russian acronym. Previously alerted and prepared for the signal they swiftly forwarded it to the silos and submarines. As they did so each of the missile locks preventing a launch was released.

Then the President lifted the phone and spoke to the G.O.U. who had been waiting on hold.

"Launch," he ordered. "Full strike".

* * *

The first American ICBM was three minutes into its flight when the third and final stage expired. It was now over 1,100 kilometres above the Earth's surface travelling at 23 times the speed of sound. It raced towards its objective covering a 7 kilometres every second.

This single missile carried three warheads with a destructive power far greater than all the bombs dropped by both sides during the second war combined, and it was just one of many.

Meanwhile in Russia hundreds of hatch doors swung open above their silos and almost immediately SS-18 rockets started emerging from mushrooming clouds of smoke and fire. At sea more missiles erupted from the surface as the ballistic missile submarines added to the barrage.

28

Revelation

The sun shall be turned into darkness, and the moon into blood, before the great and terrible day of the LORD come.
[Joel 2:31]

In America the Oval Office was in turmoil.

"They can't have fired. They can't react that fast," asserted the President, despite what he had just been told. "I've always been told it takes the Russians 15-20 minutes from the decision to fire to missiles taking off, and it hasn't even been five yet!"

Ralph was worried and was querying his archangel.

"Nothing is wrong. Everything is going according to plan."

"If you say so, archangel," he accepted unhappily. "Will the Rapture start now? The missiles will be landing soon."

"There is no such thing as Rapture, and I am not an archangel."

The look of stunned disbelief on Ralph's face distracted the President from his rant at Major Mitchell. He could only hear half the conversation but he did not like what he could hear one bit. The look on Ralph's face was starting to show signs of creeping panic.

"But you said you were. You said your name was Raphael."

"I have no name. Alex calls me Lucifer. You may refer to me by that name if you wish."

Ralph slumped on the floor.

"What did he say? When is the Rapture starting?" demanded the President, alarmed now, but Ralph was beyond speech.

Mitchell interrupted, "Sir, we have expended all the silo based missiles but we still have a third of our arsenal remaining in Trident submarines. Do you wish to launch them at Russia? Sir?"

Alex spoke to Bob: "Will it make a difference?"

"No. There are already more than enough weapons airborne to precipitate a nuclear winter, plus some other nuclear armed nations are preparing to fire."

"Tell me about the nuclear winter."

"Around a dozen extinction events have taken place in the Earth's history, five of them were particularly serious and wiped out most life on earth. The one that ended the dinosaurs as the dominant species is the best known, but was not the largest. Typically they are caused by a meteorite strike or super volcanic action putting so much fine dust in the air that it blocks out the sun and temperatures plummet. In this case nuclear explosions will supply the dust. With no sunlight plant life will start to die and with it the entire food chain. The same happens at sea as the plankton perish. If it goes on long enough all that will remain are the simple sea creatures clustered round geothermic vents on the ocean floor.

"Eventually the sun will return, new life will colonise the planet and a new dominant species will emerge. However history tells us it is never anything like what came before."

It was noisy in the room but it all sounded far away to Alex, as if at the other end of a long tunnel. Faintly she could hear the Major speaking urgently, "Sir, you can choose not to retaliate but that must be a decision, not indecision. You must issue orders. You must decide."

But the President was not listening. He was demanding answers from Ralph, but Ralph wasn't listening either. He was slumped on the floor, his back against the wall with his head in his hands weeping and the President could not help feeling a weeping angel was not a good sign. Not good at all.

"We've lost then. *I* lost," said Alex miserably. It was a statement not a question, but Bob answered all the same.

"*Yes. The Age of Man is over.*"

29

Conclusion

**For the great day of his wrath is come; and who shall be
able to stand?
[Revelation 6:17]**

Far above the Earth all that was left of the first ICBM was a Post-Boost Vehicle. It had been manoeuvring into position and now it launched the three warheads it was carrying, each wrapped up in a Re-entry Vehicle. It also launched chaff and decoys although they were superfluous as even if the Arabs had known they were coming they had nothing that could hope to stop them. Manned space craft return to Earth using big, flat heat shields to slow down, whereas these vehicles were streamlined to avoid friction and keep their approach speed high. They would cover the final four kilometres to their targets in a single second.

The three re-entry vehicles started their descent into the atmosphere, each arrowing towards a different target and arming themselves as they fell. Following behind them thousands more warheads were doing the same.

* * *

Even now it was hopeless Alex was still desperately trying to think of something. Her brother's calming words came back to her, as they had during the London Underground fire. She realised ever since she had arrived in the Oval Office she had been in a state of underlying panic and had kept grabbing at the first option to occur to her, something her brother had told her never to do. So she took a deep breath then tried to list all her options no matter how hopeless they sounded.

Eventually she spoke, slowly at first. "There was something I was going to try and it looks like I won't get another chance so…" Her dreamy voice changed abruptly becoming sharp and commanding.

"Clone Sommath and bring him here, and if I can still have a third agent bring the Old Man back. You brief him, I'll talk to the monk."

Almost instantly two black swirling clouds appeared and two men snapped into existence, adding to the consternation in the room.

The Laotian monk had a ball of sticky rice in his hand which he had just dipped in dhal sauce when the bowl, dining area and entire monastery had vanished to be replaced with a smart looking office full of Caucasians and that troublesome girl.

Keep it simple he told himself, that's the only way to maintain equilibrium. Besides he only got to eat once a day. So with commendable calm he placed the rice in his mouth and swallowed it as if nothing extraordinary had happened. That felt right. He was still sitting crossed legged on the floor and now the troublesome girl was squatting down to talk to him.

"Hi, Sommath."

"Hello Alex. I think you ought to know I asked the head monk to put the spirit house back."

"That's not important right now, but I need you to do something that is. I don't have time to explain it to you properly but what I need you to do is ignore all this and meditate. Think of nothing at all like you told me. Thoughts and images are going to pop into your head but they won't be yours and it is important you ignore them. If you don't your head will start to hurt and you will begin to feel sick. Do you understand?"

"No," he said calmly and truthfully.

Alex did not think revealing the fate of the entire human race rested on his shoulders would help his meditation much, so instead she simply said, "It will help two... people take their first steps towards enlightenment."

"Then although I do not understand I will try."

"Thank you so much."

As the monk settled down and attempted to clear his mind in the most difficult of circumstances she spoke to Bob. "Right, you first. I want you to try using his mind to process some thoughts. You said two minds in one brain caused severe problems but this man is the best there is at keeping his clear, so I want you to give it a go. Think about..." but in the tension of the moment she found her mind a blank just when she needed it most.

"Er... did the Old Man ever tell you he wished you could see the world through his eyes?"

"Yes, often."

"Then start by remembering what he was looking at when he said it." Turning to the Old Man she said, "Give him some suggestions to get started with."

So Bob looked through the monk's eyes at a sunset over the

newly finished Great Pyramid of Giza, he saw the shining pride in an artisans face as he examined the magnificent jewellery he had completed for his queen's wedding, he saw a baby screaming and tugging at its dead mother and a man run through a burning building in a futile attempt to save his daughter.

"Ooh," said Alex, "Music too. Start with the classics - Iron Maiden."

"No," said the Old Man quickly, "Try Mendelssohn beginning with Fingal's Cave. At the same time look at some of the scenes from your travels through the galaxy."

At the mention of Mendelssohn Alex made a face as if she was going to be sick but let the Old Man have his way.

So Bob started with an asteroid which failed to produce much of a reaction, but after a few variations he homed in on the ones which gave the most intense emotional responses. As the classical music soared he watched the sun flood majestically over the rough plains and crevices of a cold comet surface and saw it burst into life.

"Brother. You must see this."

So his brother did. A second clone of Sommath appeared beside the first. It was fortunate they had their eyes closed and were unaware they now had a twin as it would have been hard even for these experts in meditation not to react. Bob fired the images at him which had given the best results and for the first time the universe became not just a place they saw but a place they felt.

"This is... almost unbelievable," said Lucifer privately to Bob as he viewed the images. *"It is as if we are seeing the universe again for the first time".*

"Do you still wish to destroy human life on Earth?" asked Bob.

* * *

The first of the warheads burnt a fiery line across the desert sky. Coming in at a shallow angle Damascus was spread out below, the centre just 3 kilometres away. Set to ground burst it would cover the distance in three quarters of a second and explode immediately.

* * *

"Amazing as this is, it does nothing to change the facts. There is still a high probability of them becoming a threat to us in the future," replied Lucifer.

* * *

High above the first missile over a thousand other fiery streaks littered the sky, puzzling the few whose eyes were cast upwards. Some turned to attract the attention of those nearby but time was so short and the missiles so fast they would never have time to see it.

* * *

"I agree it is a risk. Do you think it is one worth taking?" asked Bob.

Lucifer thought about it as deeply as time would allow. Both the speed of an entity's thoughts and the speed of communications between them is blindingly fast but even so time was critically short. A precious quarter of a second slipped by.

* * *

The first missile covered another kilometre towards its target. It was over the suburbs now and just a half second from the heart of the city. When it struck there would be an explosion 13 times bigger than that suffered by Hiroshima, for this was not a primitive atom bomb but a hydrogen bomb, never before used in anger.

* * *

Lucifer tried to weigh up the benefits and the risks – difficult when both were so hard to quantify. He looked around the room where the humans appeared almost stationary such was the speed of his thoughts. Nothing they could do now would make any difference but even so most were moving pointlessly, in ultra slow motion. Having experienced the monk's mind he could now better understand their motivations and expressions, good and bad. He saw misery, arrogance, duty, truth, fear, fanaticism, regret and desperation.

Then he looked at Alex with whom he had battled these past months. Using both hands she had managed to cross her fingers four times with eight digits. Wide eyes, flushed face and trembling lips made her look more childlike and vulnerable than ever, but somehow she managed to look defiant too. Whatever happened she knew she had given it her best shot.

At last he said, *"I have decided it is a risk worth taking. They are unique and this is too valuable a resource to lose."*

There was no reluctance to abandon the work of millennia, no feelings of waste, guilt, triumph or defeat.

They acted immediately and in unison without the need for another word to pass between them.

The warheads punching fiery paths through the air towards their targets turned to dust then burnt up in the atmosphere. Life on Earth had avoided extinction by the narrowest of margins.

The debate between the entities had been inaudible to those in the room so for a while nobody realised the battle had been won.

Alex had been hoping the appearance of the second monk was a good sign but did not know for sure until Mitchell announced, "Tracking reports a fault. We can no longer locate our missiles or the Russians."

"Yeehar!" yelled Alex at the top of her voice. Then in a quieter voice she said to Bob, "Can you remove all the unlaunched ones too?"

"*Yes, if you wish.*"

"Yes please, and all the biological and chemical weapons while you are at it."

"*It has been done. Though they can all easily be rebuilt.*"

"I'm an optimist. I'm hoping they won't."

Slowly the others in the room were realising the words from Mitchell and Alex meant that somehow they had been saved from their catastrophic mistake, though they hardly dared believe it.

Suddenly Alex's demeanour changed. She swung towards the President looking unmistakably malevolent and stormed angrily towards him.

The President backed away fearfully as Alex advanced. Both Secret Service agents jumped on her in a futile attempt to stop her advance. Mitchell did the same. He had no doubt his duty was to protect the President however poor his opinion of the man.

It made no difference. Though swamped with bodies she ignored them all and marched up to the President who had retreated as far as he could and was standing with his back pressed against the wall.

"Idiot," she said, and kicked him hard in the shins. Somewhere over her left shoulder the Major started to chuckle. She turned away leaving the President holding his leg in obvious pain and took two steps back towards the centre of the room. The Major's chuckle had turned into a belly laugh and he slid off her onto the floor, unable to contain himself.

"Right," she said, her voice somewhat muffled by the Secret Service Agents still wrapped round her. "I'm sure somebody said something about a prize."

30

Confusion

Heaven and earth shall pass away... but of that day and hour knoweth no man, no, not the angels of heaven, but my Father only.
[Matthew 24:35-36]

Professor Dalton and Tom the vicar were just two of the many puzzled people watching confused reporters telling muddled stories. Newspapers were no better, their front pages consisting almost entirely of headlines, all competing equally for attention.

A nuclear war had been started for reasons that were unclear and aborted for reasons just as mysterious. Both the President and Vice President of America had resigned so for the first time ever the Speaker of the House had been called on to take over. Some countries reported all their nuclear arsenals had vanished and had gone to the highest state of military alert accusing their neighbours and expecting an attack at any moment. However with none forthcoming they were slowly starting to stand down. Meanwhile in Israel a man had popped into existence at a temple in front of the world's press, declared himself God and rambled incoherently for three quarters of an hour before vanishing again.

Professor Dalton was shaking his head in disbelief when Alex appeared out of thin air in front of him and declared, "We won. Thank you for all your help." Then she threw her arms round his neck, gave him a big kiss on the cheek and disintegrated before his eyes. After remembering to breathe the Professor smiled. He should have guessed she would be behind some of the day's amazing headlines. Probably all of them.

Alex found Tom alone in his church trying to prepare for a service he knew would be full of people looking to him for answers when he had none. He got the same treatment as the Professor but he was more shaken by it. Although he had discussed Alex's ability to instantly cross huge distances with his friend he had never actually witnessed it and found it alarming. Perhaps more unsettling, however, was the implication that he had somehow played a part in all the tumultuous events. This was not going to make his sermon any easier. He still had no idea what was going on. Feeling shaken he headed off to have a cup of tea and see if Alex had left him any biscuits.

More confused than either of them was James, her adrenaline sports mad brother. He was using the computer in his bedroom at their parent's house. The 19 year old was keen to move out but was nowhere close to achieving it since any money he earned was quickly spent on his activities, leaving him far from financially independent. He did not hear Alex come in but felt her throw her arms uncomfortably round his neck as she declared, "I missed you."

"Well, it has been twenty minutes since I saw you last," he said suspiciously, fully expecting some odious favour was about to be asked, but as always she surprised him.

"I've got a stupid question to ask you, but I want you to answer it as if it's really serious, OK?"

"OK," he said cautiously, wondering what she was up to.

"If you could see the universe but never see Mum and Dad again, would you do it?"

"You mean like travel to other planets?"

"Yes"

"You bet. I'd miss them, of course, but who could turn down something like that? It's time I moved out anyway," he said jokingly, never suspecting the effect his words would have.

She squeezed even harder and said, "Close your eyes."

He did as instructed then suddenly felt her arms gone. Not taken away, just gone. He opened his eyes to find she was nowhere to be seen. She could not have got out of the room that fast, certainly not without him hearing and the door was closed. He looked under the bed and in the cupboard but there was no sign of his frustrating little sister.

He went downstairs and found her in her own bedroom.

"How did you get out so fast?" he asked.

"Out of what?"

"My room."

"What are you talking about? It must be concussion from all that bungee jumping. Try using shorter elastic next time. I've been here all morning. I've got a pile of homework left to do that's bigger than I am," then added hastily before he could say anything, "and I'm pretty tall now. Beside I wouldn't go in your room if you paid me. It's guarded by the socks of eternal stench."

It was true, she never came in. He was at a loss but then he always was around his sister. Come to think of it she seemed to have the same effect on all men.

On the floor of her untidy room, partly covered by a torn issue of some mindless teenage girl's magazine, he could see her medal presentation box ajar with the medal spilling out. It had been awarded to her by none other than the Queen at Buckingham Palace for her bravery during the London Underground bombing. He thought about rescuing it as he, like the rest of the family, was enormously proud of her. However he did nothing as he knew if he drew attention to it she would wind him up by playing heads and tails with it, or start wondering out loud how much she could get for it on EBay. So instead he simply left and thought no more about it. It was just another puzzle from his permanently puzzling sister.

However James's clone had a quite different experience when he opened his eyes.

31

New Beginnings

**For the kingdom of heaven is as a man travelling into a
far country...
[Matthew 25:14]**

James's clone saw an impossible sight. He was no longer in his
bedroom but in a plain room surrounded by windows on all
four sides. In it were sixteen slightly bemused people. Outside
(if his eyes were to be believed and he was of the opinion they
should not) it looked very much like the surface of the moon.
The ludicrous sight gained credence from his stomach. He felt
as if he was in a plunging lift with his insides too light and too
high in his body. Completing the vision of madness were bowls
of chocolate chip cookies arranged on small shelves below each
window.

The only point of familiarity in the room was his sister
who was leaping up and down in the low gravity exclaiming
excitedly, "Look how high I can jump!"

"Where... what... when...?" tried James helplessly but he had
no idea where to begin.

"It's my prize," explained Alex, "I get to go round the universe with Bob and Lucifer. I didn't want to get lonely though, so I asked if I could bring all the past agents. Except Albert, I didn't think he would be up to it. Then I asked if you could come too and they said yes. Isn't it great?"

James tried running the 'explanation' through his head again to see if it made any more sense on the second pass - it didn't. Eventually he decided to start with a simple question. "Prize for what?"

"Saving the planet," said an old man beside him. "We are all very proud of her."

The words were nonsense but then he saw Alex squirming uncomfortably as she always did when she was praised and he knew, however impossible it sounded, it must be true.

"How did I get here?"

"Oh you are going to regret asking that," said Alex, relieved to move off the saving-the-planet conversation. "You were broken up into molecules, shot off to the moon and reassembled here. We'll do the same when we move to other planets and stars. Of course travelling to other stars will take years, but to us it will seem to happen in the blink of an eye."

"Umm…" was the most intelligent response James could come up with.

"Come and meet the others," Alex said as she grabbed his hand and hauled him off round the room. For some reason one American man she introduced as Ralph was so embarrassed he could not even meet their gaze.

"Ralph's nice, but he's a bit shy at the moment. I think he's rather cute now he's stopped scowling at me."

Ralph's expression changed to the flummoxed look that every man who spoke to Alex seemed to end up wearing. James was no stranger to it himself and shot the man a sympathetic look as he was dragged off to meet the others.

Having done the rounds Alex piped up, "Right, let's go out and play. Can you give me one of those cool NASA space suits please?"

He was not sure who she was talking to but to his surprise she was instantly enveloped in a huge, cumbersome suit that came out of nowhere. The sudden uneven weight of the built in backpack caught her off guard and she slowly toppled over backwards. Flailing on her back with arms and legs waving she looked like an upturned tortoise.

"OK, this isn't going to work. Seeing as how I'm invulnerable give me the least I can get away with. No wait, I still want to breathe air. Even if it doesn't kill me I bet sucking vacuum would be most unpleasant."

The suit vanished and was replaced by a thin one piece suit made of some kind of combined fabric and flexible mesh plus a transparent goldfish bowl style helmet.

"That's better. Now give him one and put us at the top of that," she said, pointing first to James and then to the top of a large, steep hill.

Before he could say anything he was indeed standing on the hill in a suit just like hers. He gasped involuntarily then spluttered, "But there is no air supply in these things, and we'll boil or freeze out here without more protection."

"Oh stop making such a fuss. We're invulnerable and Bob and Lucifer will handle the air and heating for us."

He could not recall ever being told who Bob and Lucifer were and they were not among the people she had introduced him to. However before he could ask Alex called out, "Sledges, please," and a pair of sledges appeared at their feet.

Alex picked up one and said, "Now are you going to stand there yapping all day or are you going to race? On the count of three…. three!" then she hopped aboard and set off down the slope.

James just stood there, completely overwhelmed by what was happening to him. Eventually two facts forced their way to the front of his confused brain. The first was that, in defiance of all logic, he had been given the opportunity to take part in the greatest adrenaline sport of his life - mankind's first ever toboggan race on the moon. The second was he was just about to lose it to his little sister.

Grabbing hold of the sledge he took the running start his sister had omitted, or at least the best he could do in the unaccustomed light gravity, and set off after her. He could see her looking back at him and hear her squealing. The question of how he could hear her without a radio in his suit could wait for now.

Bob and Lucifer watched the race, passing images and thoughts through the minds of the two copies of the obliging monk to experience the event.

"You know, I really hate the name Bob", said Bob.

Lucifer laughed for the first time since the beginning of the universe.

"I rather like the name Lucifer, I think it's cool."

The people in the room were cheering on either Alex or James. Alex was grabbing handfuls of dirt and throwing them up to fall lazily behind her while shouting, "Eat my moon dust, loser." Then she squealed as James grabbed her ankle and started pulling himself up beside her.

"Did you decide whether God exists?" asked Lucifer.

"I decided some questions don't have answers," replied Bob.

Lucifer thought about that for a while. Outside the race disintegrated into a slow tumbling mass of dust, arms, legs and sledges.

"You know, I'm looking forward to getting back out there. I think it's going to be... fun."

Author's Notes

All the people named in the story are fictitious including both Presidents. However the locations are real and the histories described are accurate except as described below.

There is a problem with the idea that in the very early universe life would naturally occur in the dense, hot, particle 'soup'. In the first second of its existence the universe consisted only of fundamental particles such as quarks, leptons and gluons, followed swiftly by protons and neutrons. None of these are well suited to making life forms. Atoms would be much better candidates but it is thought 379,000 years passed before they first made an appearance, and even then they were mostly hydrogen.

All the historical events described at the Dome of the Rock are true apart from the final earthquake and bomb that destroyed it. They allowed the building of the fictional Third Jewish Temple.

There are a large number of real Laotian Buddhist temples and monasteries but the one I describe is not. I liked the idea of meditation rooms carved into a rock face but I am not aware of any in the country that have them, so I invented one.

Reprogramming the whole United States ICBM arsenal takes

around 10 hours so it should have taken 6-7 hours repro-gramme the 2/3rds required for the story. I reduced this to 25 minutes so as not to slow the pace.

There is huge debate amongst the End Times movement as to what signs need to be fulfilled, which ones have already taken place, and the sequence of events. In particular whether the Rapture takes place before, during or after the Tribulation. Some think all the prophecies have been fulfilled already. The events and sequence I have chosen are just one of the many views out there.

I used 'quantum entanglement' as a means of instant commu-nication. While it has been successfully demonstrated in the laboratory and the effect is instantaneous over any distance it is a widely believed that we will never successfully manage to use it to send meaningful information, thus preventing breaking the rule that nothing can travel faster than the speed of light.

The precise details of how the US Football and Russian Black Cases function are meant to be secret, though most of it has been leaked. Gaps in the known details were filled with best guesses.

The story was written in British English so if you read the book in the US or elsewhere I hope you did not mind differences in the way some words are spelt and the occasional odd turn of phrase.

I hope you enjoyed the story. I have sketched out a sequel which will be a full length novel. Whether it sees the light of day depends on how this book is received. So if you want to know what happens next to Alex, Bob and Lucifer please let me know in your reviews.

Printed in Great Britain
by Amazon